A Secret in Time

As Nancy placed the clock on her dresser, she
heard a distinct rattle. That's funny, she thought.
I've never heard that noise before.

She shook the clock slightly, and again she heard
the rattle. There was no mistake—the noise was
coming from inside. Placing it on the bed, Nancy
opened the glass door enclosing the clock face.
Then she used the screwdriver attachment on
her pocketknife to remove the screws around the
face. Nancy pulled off the two hands of the clock
and swung the face open. A small object fell onto
her comforter.

As she saw the gleam of red and green gems,
Nancy realized what had been inside the clock.
It was the missing brooch!

Nancy Drew
Mystery Stories

Available from MINSTREL Books

100

NANCY® DREW

A SECRET IN TIME

CAROLYN KEENE

A MINSTREL® BOOK

PUBLISHED BY POCKET BOOKS

New York   London   Toronto   Sydney   Tokyo   Singapore

A MINSTREL PAPERBACK *ORIGINAL*

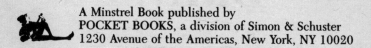 A Minstrel Book published by
POCKET BOOKS, a division of Simon & Schuster
1230 Avenue of the Americas, New York, NY 10020

ISBN: 0-671-69286-0

First Minstrel Books printing April 1991

10 9 8 7 6 5 4 3 2 1

Cover art by Aleta Jenks

Printed in the U.S.A.

Contents

A SECRET
IN TIME

1

Time for Trouble

"It's funny that we're making a special trip just to see your clock," Bess Marvin said to her friend Nancy Drew. "I mean, we can see it any time sitting on your dresser."

Nancy smiled as she turned her blue convertible sports car into the teachers' parking lot at River Heights High School. "You know what else is weird?" Nancy asked. "Parking in the teachers' lot. It wasn't that long ago that we were seniors here."

"We would have been towed away in two seconds back then," Bess said. "Kind of feels like we're getting away with something."

Through her dark glasses, Nancy's deep blue eyes surveyed the lines of parked cars in the lot. "Looks like everyone in town showed up for the antiques expo. We'll be lucky to get a space. Wait, I see one.

This is going to be tight. . . ." She expertly maneuvered her sports car into a narrow parking space, and the two girls got out.

"Whew! It's hot." Bess squinted into the summer sunlight as she and Nancy hurried across the asphalt toward a side entrance to the building.

Shorter and with a slightly rounder build than Nancy, Bess had to hurry to keep up. Grabbing an elastic band from the outside pocket of her purse, Bess twisted her straight blond hair into a makeshift bun to get it off her neck. Nancy's reddish blond hair was already pulled back in a neat French braid. She was wearing white shorts and a navy T-shirt.

The girls entered the high school and made their way down the cool, dim hall toward the gymnasium, where the antiques expo was being held. Half a dozen other people were heading in the same direction.

"By the way," said Bess, smoothing her blue cotton sundress, "don't get me wrong about the clock. I think it's great that Mr. Gordon wants to feature it in his exhibit. You're not going to let him sell it, are you?"

Nancy's eyes widened. "Of course not! That's a memento of my very first case. It means more to me than anything else I own."

Though Nancy was only eighteen years old, she was already an experienced detective. With the help of Bess and Bess's cousin, George Fayne, Nancy had solved many baffling cases in River Heights and all over the world. In her first case, Nancy had helped some poor families collect large sums of money they had inherited. She had discovered a tiny notebook and key hidden inside an old clock, and those clues led her to a secret will that left the savings of a rich old man, Josiah Crowley, to his poor relatives. In gratitude, the heirs had given the clock to Nancy as a keepsake.

After keeping perfect time for quite a while, the clock had begun to run slow. Nancy had taken it to a local antique-store owner, Henry Gordon, who was also an expert at clock repair. Mr. Gordon told Nancy he had never seen a clock quite like it, and he asked her where she'd gotten it. When Nancy told him the story, he was so impressed that he asked her permission to exhibit the clock at the antiques expo. Then Mr. Gordon had invited Nancy to come to the show to see it on display.

"Looks as if this is a pretty popular event," said Bess, as she and Nancy approached the gymnasium. "Reminds me of all those high-school dances."

A large crowd was milling about outside the entrance. In front of the doors, men and women at long tables were collecting admission fees.

When Nancy and Bess reached one of the tables, a pudgy woman pushed a lined piece of paper toward them. "Please give us your name and address," she said. "We'd like to put you on our mailing list for future expos."

3

After they'd paid and signed in, the girls entered the gym.

"Wow!" Bess exclaimed, pausing just inside the doors. "Look at this place."

Nancy followed her friend's gaze. The gym had been completely transformed. The bleachers were still set up against one wall, but the rest of the huge, open room was filled with row after row of exhibits. Some were long tables covered with jewelry, glassware, and small household objects. There were also stands displaying all kinds of artwork and clothing from earlier eras. Some of the exhibits were much larger, featuring groupings of furniture and, in one case, an antique car.

"It's hard to believe this is the same place where we used to dribble basketballs and do jumping jacks," Nancy observed.

"Ugh. Don't remind me," Bess said with a shiver. "I like it much better this way."

Nancy laughed. Athletics had never been one of Bess's favorite activities. Nancy knew her friend would rather shop than do push-ups any day.

"We'll never find Mr. Gordon," Bess said, a frown creasing her brow.

"Sure we will." Nancy grabbed a map from a pile right inside the door and scanned it. "Here's Mr. Gordon's exhibit," she announced. "Past Perfect is the name of his store. He's at booth six."

They were halfway down the second row when Bess

4

pulled Nancy toward a glass display case. "Do you mind if we just look for a minute?" she asked. "I'd like to check out the jewelry."

"Take your time," Nancy said. "I'm not in any hurry."

As she followed Bess over to a jewelry display, Nancy had to sidestep a tall, slender woman dressed dramatically in a black minidress and a small black hat. A gauzy white scarf was looped around her neck, and she wore dark glasses, even though she was indoors. Nancy glanced curiously at the woman. There was something oddly familiar about her. But before she could figure out where she'd seen her before, Bess was pulling her over to the display case.

"Oh, look at this stuff!" Bess exclaimed, her blue eyes gleaming.

Inside the case, sparkling antique watches, rings, bracelets, and brooches were lined up in orderly rows on a piece of black velvet. "It's a good thing I didn't bring my credit card," Bess went on, pointing at a white gold ring with a cluster of tiny pearls. "That's gorgeous. I wonder how much it costs."

A thin man behind the counter peered at Bess over large horn-rimmed glasses that sat low on his nose. He was in his mid-thirties and wore his light brown hair cut short. "It's very expensive," he said. "*Very* expensive."

Nancy was surprised at the man's tone. A comment such as that would turn away more business than it

5

would attract, she thought. Of course, she and Bess weren't seriously planning to buy the ring, but the man didn't know that. Nancy glanced at the sign in front of the man's exhibit. It read Russell Brown Antiques.

"Mr. Brown?" Nancy asked the man, raising her eyebrows.

When he nodded, Nancy asked, "How old is this pearl ring? It's so pretty."

"It's a rare piece from the turn of the century. There aren't many like it." Mr. Brown took a pair of amethyst earrings out of a case to show a customer, and Bess and Nancy looked at some of the other pieces of jewelry.

"I didn't even want to hear how much that ring cost," Bess said under her breath.

"You probably would have fainted right on the spot if he had told you," Nancy replied, and both girls laughed.

Nancy glanced at the other customers at Mr. Brown's booth—a handful of women and a big man with an orange T-shirt stretched over his fat stomach. "I wonder what these people think of Mr. Brown's prices," she whispered to Bess.

Bess put back the necklace of semiprecious stones she'd been admiring. "They seem way out of line to me."

Nancy spotted Henry Gordon across the aisle and pointed him out to Bess. Even in the crush of people,

6

Mr. Gordon stood out. While everyone else was dressed in casual summer clothing, Mr. Gordon looked as if he'd stepped out of an English novel. He was wearing an old suit with a matching vest and tiny round eyeglasses with metal frames. His gray hair was combed back, and Nancy could see the gold chain of a pocket watch tucked in his vest. Gordon noticed Nancy and Bess and waved them over to his booth.

"It's a madhouse!" he shouted as the girls pushed through the crowd toward him.

"I guess we're not the only ones with a passion for the past," Nancy said, grinning. "Mr. Gordon, this is my friend Bess Marvin."

"Very pleased to meet you," Mr. Gordon said, shaking Bess's hand.

"I know your assistant, Lydia Newkirk," Bess volunteered. "She grew up down the street from me. I haven't seen her since she went away to college a few years ago. I heard she was back, though, and working for you."

"A singular young woman," Mr. Gordon said, smiling fondly. "And a great help to me."

"Is Lydia here today?" Bess asked. "I'd love to say hello."

Mr. Gordon nodded and gestured vaguely at the crowd. "Somewhere. She's been working hard all morning, so I gave her some time to shop."

"I'll bet she's looking for costumes," Bess said. She turned to Nancy. "You remember Lydia, don't you?

7

She's the one who liked to dress up in outfits from different times."

"Oh, yes," Nancy said after thinking a moment. "I remember seeing her once wearing long white gloves and carrying a parasol."

Bess giggled. "That's Lydia, all right."

"She's been a big help to my business," Mr. Gordon said. "Customers come into my shop just to see what she'll be wearing. Now," he added, ushering the girls to a round wooden table in the center of his display, "I'm sure you're eager to see my exhibit's special attraction. I've brought mostly smaller pieces today, so your clock is truly the centerpiece."

Nancy smiled when she saw the clock standing alone on a mahogany table. A tall mantel clock with a square face covered by a glass door, it was topped with five round crystal ornaments. The wood encasing the clock was polished to a high gloss, and its brass fittings gleamed brightly.

In front of the clock sat a framed card with an inscription:

English mantel clock, circa 1892
Owned by Nancy Drew, River Heights
   Originally owned by Josiah Crowley, a local millionaire. In his later years, Crowley hid a notebook and key, which led to his second and final will, behind the clock's face. Only through the efforts of Nancy Drew, River Heights's famous

8

detective, was the will discovered and Crowley's inheritance given to his rightful heirs.

"Pretty impressive, Nancy," Bess said proudly after reading the card.

Nancy blushed when she read the part about River Heights's famous detective. Then she noticed that the clock face was ajar to show the empty space behind it.

"It was very nice of you to put out that sign," she said to Mr. Gordon, "but it really wasn't necessary. I'm sure the clock is pretty ordinary."

"But its owner isn't," said Mr. Gordon. "And the clock is now a part of the history of our town. I consider it an important piece."

"Well," Nancy said, still feeling embarrassed, "I think Bess and I should go—"

"Bess!" cried a high-pitched female voice. Nancy and Bess turned to see a tall young woman in a full-skirted dress made of lavender-flowered cotton. The sleeveless top was fitted and tied at the waist with a purple sash, and the long skirt was made fuller by the petticoats underneath. She wore a wide-brimmed straw hat that had a ring of lilacs tucked into the band, and her dark brown hair was braided down to the middle of her back.

"You look gorgeous!" Bess exclaimed, hugging the woman. "Like a character from an old movie. Are you really my long-lost neighbor, Lydia Newkirk, or a flash from the past?"

9

"All of the above," said Lydia excitedly. "How have you been, Bess?"

"Great," Bess told her. "It's been so long. When you went away to college, you really went away."

Lydia shrugged. "I traveled during the summers," she explained. "But now I'm back to stay."

"You remember Nancy Drew, don't you?" Bess asked.

"Of course I do," Lydia replied, nodding to Nancy. "You two were always inseparable. But where's the third musketeer?"

Bess laughed. "You must mean my cousin George. She's got a temporary job driving a Frosty Freeze ice cream truck. It's a really great deal for me, since George is so generous."

Nancy couldn't help smiling. Despite her best efforts at dieting, Bess always seemed to be a little overweight.

"I'm glad to see you haven't changed," Bess continued, looking at Lydia's outfit enviously. "How do you afford all these great clothes?"

Lydia shrugged. "They don't cost as much as you'd think. I usually get them at thrift shops."

"Well, you must be having a field day with all the costumes around here," Bess said. "Have you bought a new outfit?"

Lydia shrugged. "I didn't see anything I liked. Well, look, I'd better get back to work."

"We were just about to explore," said Bess. "Maybe I'll see you in the neighborhood."

"That would be great. I'm living with my parents again, at least for a while," Lydia said.

"Nice to see you, Lydia," Nancy said as she and Bess left the booth. "Mr. Gordon, I'll be back to pick up the clock at the end of the day."

Mr. Gordon, busy with a customer, gave them a wave.

"Lydia's great," Bess said as they pushed back into the crowd. "I've always admired her."

"She's certainly not afraid to be different," Nancy agreed. "So, what do you want to see first?"

Bess pointed to a furniture display of a sleekly designed 1930s living room. "I just love that style," Bess sighed. "It's so sophisticated and—" Bess was interrupted by a nearby shout.

"Help!" called a voice that sounded vaguely familiar to Nancy. "Help! Police!"

Nancy turned in the direction of the shout and saw Russell Brown flailing an arm, his face bright red.

"What's wrong?" Nancy called, running toward his booth.

Mr. Brown didn't seem to hear or see Nancy. His head turned frantically in all directions, and there was a look of dismay on his flushed face. "Call the police. I've been robbed!" he cried.

2

The Old Clock Strikes Again

Bess followed right behind Nancy to Russell Brown's booth. Henry Gordon arrived at the same moment.

"I never should have allowed that Jennings woman to persuade me to display here!" Mr. Brown fumed. "For this I paid a two-hundred-dollar exhibition fee? I ought to sue Ms. Jennings."

"Who's Ms. Jennings?" Nancy asked calmly, noticing that a crowd was beginning to gather.

"The woman who is supposed to run this event," Mr. Brown fumed. "She's a well-known socialite in River Heights."

"I'm sure it's not her fault you were robbed," Nancy said. "Why don't you try to calm down and tell me what was stolen?"

"It's a one-of-a-kind piece," he said, becoming more agitated. "My rose brooch. It's a very expensive

12

pin worth fifty thousand dollars! And it's irreplace-able."

"Could you describe it?" Nancy asked.

"It's a rose, done entirely in precious gems. The petals are made of rubies, and the stem and leaves are emeralds. I never should have brought it here."

Before Nancy could question Mr. Brown further, a heavyset middle-aged police officer broke through the crowd. Her notebook was already open.

"I'm Sergeant Margaret Rudinsky," she said. "What is the problem?"

"A priceless antique was stolen from my collec-tion," Mr. Brown said, turning to the sergeant.

Rudinsky clicked the top of her ballpoint pen and began to write. "What was its estimated value?" she asked.

Nancy stepped back to let the officer do her job. She was relieved that she didn't have to deal with Mr. Brown any longer. He was obviously quite upset. She hadn't come to the show looking for another case. It would be nice, for once, Nancy thought, to relax and enjoy my summer. Maybe tomorrow Bess and I can go swimming at the lake.

Still, Nancy couldn't help listening as Brown de-scribed the brooch for the second time. "My other mistake," he went on, "was unlocking the case to show someone a bracelet. I turned my back for just a second, and the next time I looked, the brooch was gone."

"How long ago was this?" Sergeant Rudinsky asked.

"Not five minutes—" Brown was about to say something more, but the police officer cut him off by raising her walkie-talkie to her mouth. "Brody, do you read me?" she asked.

A man's voice crackled over the walkie-talkie. "Officer Brody here."

"Seal the area," Sergeant Rudinsky said. "There has been a robbery. No one is to leave the building. Over."

Rudinsky pressed a button, then spoke again into her walkie-talkie. "RH Central, this is Rudinsky at the high school. There's been a robbery. The area has been sealed. Request backup units."

"Roger, Rudinsky," came a staticky female voice over the walkie-talkie. "They're on their way."

Nancy turned as an attractive woman in a red suit emerged from the crowd and approached Sergeant Rudinsky. Her black hair was slicked back into a tight bun, and she wore large pearl earrings.

"I'm Mary Lou Jennings, coordinator of this event," the woman said.

Nancy recognized Ms. Jennings when she saw her. She was a prominent woman in town who had organized many charities and social functions.

Sergeant Rudinsky told Ms. Jennings about the theft. Then she asked, "Is there a loudspeaker system here? We should make an announcement so everyone knows what's going on. We'll have to search every person in the room."

"Of course," said Ms. Jennings. "I'll take care of it." She hurried past the rows of exhibits to a microphone at one side of the gymnasium. Even though she was wearing high-heeled black patent-leather pumps, she deftly climbed up three rows of bleachers so that everyone in the gym could see her.

"Attention, please," Ms. Jennings said, and paused as the crowd looked up toward her. "There's been a robbery," she continued. "The police have sealed the gymnasium and will need to conduct a search. This might take some time, so I apologize for any inconvenience."

A collective groan rose from the floor, followed by the loud buzz of voices.

Nancy looked around at the huge, bustling crowd. "Some time could mean the better part of the day, with all these people," she said to Bess. "And the thief might already have escaped."

Bess nodded. "I saw a snack bar near the entrance to the gym. If we're going to be here for a long time, I'd better stock up. I noticed they had some chocolate croissants."

Nancy had to laugh. Bess's mind was never far from food. "Well, I don't know about you, but I'm going to let them search me now and get it over with."

Unfortunately, almost a hundred other people had the same idea. A long line had already formed by the bleachers, turning at the corner of the gym around the perimeter of the exhibits. Standing on tiptoe,

Nancy looked over the crowd and saw Sergeant Rudinsky climbing up the bleachers to join Mary Lou Jennings.

To the right of the bleachers, a young police officer was standing by the blocked entrance. As Nancy watched, he lifted his walkie-talkie to his ear, nodded, and opened the doors to allow four more officers in. When they spotted Sergeant Rudinsky, the officers headed toward her. Nancy couldn't hear what the sergeant said, but she could see the officers nodding. Then they stationed themselves along the floor in front of the bleachers.

Sergeant Rudinsky took the microphone from Ms. Jennings. "We'll try to get through this as quickly as possible," she said. "When an officer has released you, please proceed to the exit."

As Nancy headed for the end of the ever-growing line, Bess turned toward the snack bar. "Want me to get you anything?" she asked.

It would be an hour's wait, at least. Shooting her friend a smile, Nancy said, "I'll take a chocolate croissant."

Two hours later the croissant was a dim memory. But at last Nancy reached the front of the line. Sergeant Rudinsky efficiently patted Nancy down, then went through her purse. "Thank you," the officer said. "You're free to go." She gestured toward the gym doors on her right. "Through there, please. We can't have anyone lingering."

Suddenly Nancy remembered her clock. She couldn't leave without it. "I have something on display that I'd like to take with me," she said to Sergeant Rudinsky. "Could I get it?"

The sergeant gave Nancy a careful once-over and asked, "Which display?" Nancy told her, and Sergeant Rudinsky spoke briefly into her walkie-talkie. "I guess it's okay," she said, clicking off the walkie-talkie. "That booth has already been searched. It's clean."

Nancy noticed that the police were carefully controlling the traffic of people through the gym. The people and displays that hadn't yet been searched were being kept separate from those that had. It made a lot of sense, Nancy realized. Otherwise, whoever stole the brooch could hand it to someone the police had already searched.

Bess was next in line, so Nancy headed back to Henry Gordon's booth. Mr. Gordon and Lydia were packing the antiques into cardboard boxes. In one of the boxes, Nancy could see the top of her clock poking up through a nest of Styrofoam chips.

"I'm sorry about the way this turned out," Nancy said to Mr. Gordon. "I guess this wasn't very good for business."

Mr. Gordon sighed. "It's a shame when you can't trust people long enough to turn your back."

Nancy nodded. "Thank you for doing such a beautiful job on my clock," she told him. "How much do I owe you for repairing it?"

"No charge," Mr. Gordon said.

Nancy started to protest, but Mr. Gordon held up his hand. "It took me less than five minutes to fix the winding mechanism. And your clock was a wonderful conversation piece. It attracted a lot of people to my booth. Despite what happened today, our sales were excellent."

Lydia smiled at Nancy from behind some cardboard boxes. "Don't argue with the man."

Nancy laughed. "Thanks, Mr. Gordon. That's really generous of you. Well, if you're done with the clock, I guess I'll take it home."

"Now, why should you go to the trouble of lugging it home?" Gordon asked, patting the box. "Let me deliver it to your house tomorrow. We'll be making a run in your neighborhood—"

"No," Nancy said quickly. "It's enough that you're not charging me for the clock. The least I can do is take it home myself."

"It's really no trouble," he said.

"No," Nancy repeated. "I can do it. My car is parked right outside."

Mr. Gordon shrugged. "Well, at least let me seal the box for you." Taking a tape gun from a tool chest, he fastened down the cardboard flaps.

"Thanks," Nancy said, lifting the box.

As Nancy met Bess at the doors, she heard the familiar sound of Russell Brown's frantic voice. Peering over the top of the box, Nancy saw he was with Sergeant Rudinsky.

18

"What do you mean, everyone is clean?" he demanded. "Someone here has *got* to have my brooch."

"It's possible the thief escaped before we conducted the search," Sergeant Rudinsky said calmly. "But I assure you the police department will do everything possible to recover your property."

"Everything possible?" Brown yelled. "This never should have happened in the first place! That brooch was worth thousands."

"Take it up with Chief McGinnis," Sergeant Rudinsky said stiffly. Then she walked away.

Bess shook her head. "I guess Mr. Brown is pretty upset."

"Yeah," Nancy agreed. "But that brooch was worth a lot of money."

"Well, at least it's not *your* headache," Bess said. "This is one case you won't have to solve."

"That's exactly what I was thinking," Nancy said. She shifted the cardboard box in her arms. "This thing is heavy. Let's get out of here."

Following the crowd, Nancy and Bess made their way down the hallways to the exit. Then they threaded through the line of slow-moving cars trying to get out of the parking lot. Finally, after what seemed like forever, they edged out of the lot and onto the street, the clock sitting on the back seat of Nancy's car.

"What an afternoon," Bess said, putting on her sunglasses. "Phew!"

Nancy felt the cool breeze on her face as the car

19

sped along the road. "Maybe tomorrow we should try for something a little more fun," she said. "How about the lake?"

"Sure," Bess replied. "I've been dying for an opportunity to show off my new bathing suit."

"Maybe George can come with us. Is she working tomorrow?" Nancy asked.

"I'll give her a call," Bess replied.

A few minutes later Nancy dropped Bess off at her house and drove home.

"Hi, Hannah!" she called as she carried the box inside. Hannah Gruen, the Drews' housekeeper, had lived with Nancy and Nancy's father, Carson Drew, ever since Nancy's mother died, when Nancy was three. Hannah was one of the family, and Nancy couldn't imagine what their household would be like without her.

A woman in her sixties with graying hair poked her head out of the kitchen door and smiled. "Did you have fun at the expo?" Hannah asked.

"It's a long story," Nancy said, heading for the stairs with her box.

"What's that supposed to mean?" Hannah asked. "There wasn't any trouble, was there?"

Nancy smiled at the concerned note in the housekeeper's voice. Hannah was always watching out for Nancy. She didn't like it when Nancy's cases put her in danger.

"Don't worry, Hannah," Nancy called over her shoulder. "This time it doesn't have anything to do

20

with me. I'm just going to put my clock back on the dresser. Then I'll help you with dinner."

Nancy went up to her room and placed the box on her bed. Then, after slicing the tape with her pocketknife, she carefully lifted the clock out of the box. Even in the fading afternoon light, it gleamed like new. Mr. Gordon had done a thorough job of restoring it.

As Nancy placed the clock on her dresser, she heard a distinct rattle. That's funny, she thought. I've never heard that noise before.

She shook the clock slightly, and again she heard the rattle. There was no mistake—the noise was coming from inside. But how could this be? Nancy wondered, thinking that Mr. Gordon was a very careful man. He never would have returned the clock to Nancy if a piece inside were loose.

Placing the clock on the bed, Nancy opened the glass door. Then she used the screwdriver attachment on her pocketknife to remove the screws around the clock face. Nancy pulled off the two hands of the clock and swung the face open. A small object fell onto her comforter.

As she saw the gleam of red and green gems, Nancy realized what had been inside the clock. It was the missing rose brooch!

3

A Very Healthy Suspect

For several moments Nancy stared at the beautiful brooch lying on her comforter. Though it was flat, it really did look like a rose. The petals were outlined in gold and filled in with tiny rubies. The graceful stem was formed with emeralds. A single emerald leaf extended from the stem.

No wonder Mr. Brown had been so upset, Nancy thought. The brooch was breathtaking and clearly very valuable. He'd certainly be happy to hear she'd found it. Nancy frowned as she wondered who could have hidden the brooch inside her clock.

It was easy for Nancy to figure out why the piece of jewelry had been stashed. Whoever had tried to steal it hadn't gotten out of the gym before the police began their search. In the confusion while everyone was lining up, the thief had hidden the brooch inside

22

the clock, planning to retrieve it later. After all, Mr. Gordon had displayed the clock with the face open to reveal where the notebook from her first case had been hidden. Anyone could have dropped the brooch inside and closed the face.

It wasn't as easy to answer the more important question of who the thief was. Nancy tried to recall the faces of the people she'd seen near Russell Brown's display when he had cried out. There had been a couple of women and a heavy man, but she couldn't recall any specific features. With a sigh, Nancy realized the thief could have been almost anyone.

Taking a handkerchief from her dresser drawer, Nancy wrapped up the brooch. She was careful not to smudge any fingerprints that might remain on it. Then she lifted the receiver of the telephone extension in her room and dialed the number of the River Heights police station.

"Chief McGinnis, please," she said to the officer who answered. "It's Nancy Drew."

The chief of police got on the phone right away. "Don't tell me you're on another case," he said.

Though Nancy couldn't see him, she could tell Chief McGinnis was smiling. He had often worked with Nancy's father, Carson Drew, who was a lawyer in River Heights. And Nancy herself had worked with the police chief on several cases.

"Not exactly," Nancy replied. "But I think I may have solved a case I wasn't even working on. I found the piece of jewelry your officers were looking for at the antiques expo."

"Already?" Chief McGinnis sounded surprised and pleased. "That's got to be a record, even for you. How did you find it?"

Nancy told him about discovering the brooch inside her clock. Then she explained her theory of how it might have ended up there. "Do you want me to bring it to the station?" she asked.

She heard Chief McGinnis sigh. "I'll tell you," he said, "we're going crazy here right now. We've got a holdup at the liquor store, a missing child, and a hit-and-run. Since the brooch has been found and is in good hands, I think we can wait until tomorrow. Have you got a safe place to store it?"

"My father's safe," Nancy said. "It's heavy-duty."

"Good. Put the brooch away and come by the station late tomorrow morning. Meanwhile, I'll call the owner and tell him we've got it. I'll see you and the brooch tomorrow."

After Nancy hung up, she carefully lifted the handkerchief-wrapped brooch and took it downstairs to her father's study. She unlocked the safe, placed the piece inside, then closed the door securely. There was just one more thing she had to do. She walked down the hall and paused outside the kitchen door.

"Hannah?" The housekeeper turned from the pie-crust she was preparing, and Nancy said, "I'd like to make a quick visit to Bess and George. I'll be back in time to help with dinner."

"Go ahead," Hannah said. "I wasn't going to start for another half hour at least."

"Thanks," Nancy said, giving Hannah a kiss.

Nancy found her two best friends sitting on the porch in front of George's house. As Nancy walked up the front path, she saw that the girls were eating red, white, and blue Popsicles.

"Are those Frosty Freeze specials?" Nancy asked as she climbed the porch steps.

"It's Fr-fr-fr-fr-frosty good," George Fayne said, reciting the company's advertising slogan. Her long, lean frame was stretched out in a wicker chair. She still wore her Frosty Freeze uniform, a smock and a white nylon baseball cap, which covered most of her short brown hair.

It was funny, Nancy thought, how George and Bess were so different, even though they were cousins. Taller and slimmer than Bess, George had the build of a natural athlete. She also had a practical, down-to-earth way of looking at things. It was nice that none of their differences got in the way of their close friendship.

"Want one?" Bess offered, removing a Popsicle from an ice-filled cooler next to her chair. "They have only seventy calories."

"I'm too excited to think about food right now,"

Nancy said, sitting down on the top step. "You'll never guess what I found."

"Uh-oh," Bess said. "Why do I have the feeling that we're not going swimming tomorrow?"

"You found the brooch," George guessed, her brown eyes gleaming. "Bess told me what happened this afternoon. I knew you'd figure it out."

Nancy shook her head. "I didn't do anything except try to put my clock back on the dresser. I heard a rattle, and when I looked inside, I found the brooch." She grinned. "It wasn't exactly brilliant detective work."

"The old clock strikes again," Bess said dramatically, taking another bite of her Popsicle.

"So do you have any idea who put it there?" George asked.

Nancy shook her head. "It could have been anyone."

"Anyone could have *stolen* the brooch," Bess pointed out. "But it would have been much harder to hide it inside the clock when Mr. Gordon was right there."

"That's true," agreed Nancy. "But after Russell Brown let everyone know what happened, there was so much confusion that the thief may have had the chance. And Mr. Gordon was right behind us when we went to help Mr. Brown, remember?"

George leaned forward. "So since he was with you, he probably didn't have a chance to hide the brooch."

"Well, he might have had time, if he had gone

directly to the clock after he stole the brooch. He was the person with the best chance to hide it, except for—"

"Don't even think it!" Bess cried. "I know what's going through your mind, Nancy, and there's no way it's possible."

"I know you've always admired Lydia," Nancy said, "but she's got as good a chance of being guilty as anyone else. Think about it. Lydia said she was shopping during the time the brooch was stolen, but she didn't return with any packages. And she was alone at Mr. Gordon's booth right afterward. She would have had the perfect opportunity to hide the brooch inside the clock."

"Well, what about Henry Gordon?" Bess said. "He knew about the space behind the clock face."

"So did Lydia and anyone else who looked at the clock," Nancy said. "Remember what was printed on the card? And the clock face was open."

Bess thought for a moment. "Mr. Gordon's the only other person who was alone with the clock. And you told me he seemed awfully eager to deliver the clock to you himself rather than have you take it. Maybe he wanted to remove the brooch before he gave the clock back."

Nancy had to admit Bess had a point. "I'll put him on my list," she said. "Along with several hundred other suspects. Chief McGinnis wants to see the brooch tomorrow morning. Do either of you want to go with me? Maybe we can go swimming afterward."

"I've got to work," George said. "But let me know what happens. You can call me on my new mobile phone." Reaching down beside her on the porch floor, George pulled out a black leather case and removed a slim black phone with an antenna. "Isn't this great?" she asked. "I can call anyone in the world on this. And other people can call me, wherever I am."

"She hasn't talked about anything else since she bought that thing," Bess said, rolling her eyes. "I'm surprised she doesn't keep it under her pillow at night."

"No way," said George, laughing at Bess. "I recharge it at night. Here's my number if you ever need it, Nan." George reached into the pocket of her Frosty Freeze smock and pulled out a little card on which she'd already written her number. Nancy took the card and put it in her wallet.

"I'll go with you, Nancy," Bess offered. "What time?"

"The chief said late morning, but maybe we could go over to Past Perfect beforehand. I'd like to question Lydia and Mr. Gordon. I'll pick you up at ten, okay?" Nancy glanced at her watch. "Oops, it's later than I thought. I promised Hannah I'd help her with dinner." Getting to her feet, Nancy ran lightly down the porch steps. "'Bye, George." she called over her shoulder. "See you in the morning, Bess."

* * *

Nancy loved entering Henry Gordon's store. Walking into Past Perfect was almost like stepping into another time. Tall wardrobes stood among rolltop desks, four-poster beds, and high-backed armchairs.

At the sound of the door chimes Mr. Gordon appeared from the back of the store. He was wearing the same tiny round spectacles he'd had on at the antiques expo, and another old-fashioned suit with a vest. At the high school, he'd looked out of place, but in his store he fit in perfectly.

"Good morning, girls." He greeted Nancy and Bess warmly, but Nancy thought she detected some worry in his eyes. "Is anything wrong with the clock?"

"Not exactly," Nancy told him. "You might say I got it back in even better condition than I expected."

Mr. Gordon smiled. "That's my policy, to return things better than I received them."

Nancy glanced around the store. "Are we alone?"

Mr. Gordon nodded, looking a little puzzled.

Nancy reached into her purse and pulled out her handkerchief, gently opening the folds to reveal the rose brooch. "I found this inside the clock when I got home."

Mr. Gordon gasped. "But how—"

"That's what we'd like to know," Nancy said. She rewrapped the brooch and put it into her purse.

"You don't think I . . . ?" Mr. Gordon began, his face reddening.

"I'm not accusing anyone," Nancy said quickly. "I

was just wondering if you could tell me who was watching the clock at the expo, and if there was ever a time when it wasn't being watched.''

"Lydia and I were both at the booth the entire time," Gordon said, "except when Lydia took her break, and when I joined you at Brown's booth after he discovered his brooch was missing." The antique dealer became thoughtful. "You don't think Lydia . . .''

"I don't know," Nancy answered. "But we can't rule anyone out.''

Mr. Gordon stared into space over Nancy's shoulder, frowning as if trying to make up his mind about something. "You know," he said finally, "I wasn't going to mention this, but something very strange happened here at the shop last night after I left. When I arrived this morning, I noticed that some of my papers had been rearranged. And all the boxes brought back from the expo had been opened. Nothing was taken, though.''

"Was there any sign of forced entry?" Nancy asked.

He nodded. "The window to my office was open. I'm sure I closed it last night before I left.''

"Don't you have an alarm system?" Nancy asked, glancing at all the valuable things in the store.

Mr. Gordon shook his head. "Maybe I'm too old-fashioned," he admitted, "but I still trust people.'' Then his expression brightened. "But if someone *did* break in, that rules out Lydia. She's got a key.''

"She could have made it look like a break-in," Nancy pointed out. What she didn't say was that Mr. Gordon, too, could have faked a break-in to make himself look less suspicious.

"Speaking of Lydia," Bess said, "where is she?"

"She called in sick today," Mr. Gordon said. "She has some sort of flu."

"Hmmm." Nancy couldn't help wondering if there might be a connection between the break-in and Lydia's sudden illness. "Do you mind if I take a look at the window?" she asked.

Mr. Gordon led her and Bess through the store and into his office. Boxes lined one wall, and antique prints hung on the other three walls. The window was just above a small wooden desk.

Nancy went over and looked at the window. "I see the latch is closed now," she said to Mr. Gordon. "Did you lock it last night?"

He gave her a sheepish look. "To be perfectly honest, I don't remember. But I can tell you I will from now on. And I'm going to get an alarm system, too."

Nancy unlocked the window and opened it, but she didn't notice any scratch marks on the paint or the windowsill. The entry hadn't been forced.

Just then the quiet in the shop was shattered by the ringing of bells. Nearby, a grandfather clock chimed eleven o'clock, and the sound was echoed by smaller timepieces all over the store.

31

"We'd better go," said Nancy. "We've got to take the brooch to the police station. I hope you don't mind if I tell Chief McGinnis about your break-in."

"Not at all," Mr. Gordon replied. "Please keep me informed."

"We will," Nancy promised.

"I feel so bad even considering Mr. Gordon a suspect," Nancy said as she pulled her sports car away from the antique dealer's shop.

"How do you think *I* feel about Lydia?" Bess asked.

"Don't worry," Nancy said. "For all we know, Lydia had nothing to do with it. We'll talk to her as soon as she gets over her flu."

At that moment Nancy glimpsed something that startled her. Instinctively she began to put on the brakes, but a loud honk from the car behind her forced her to keep on going.

"Are you okay?" Bess asked, lurching with the sudden movements of the car. "What was that all about?"

Nancy didn't want to say anything until she was certain. But she could have sworn she'd just seen a tall young woman dressed in a 1920s-style flapper dress. The beaded blue dress was short, and the woman wore a small hat with a blue feather sticking out. She was in the doorway of an empty store, talking with a man in a business suit. It had happened so fast that Nancy wasn't sure whom she'd seen. But if she was correct, that flapper was Lydia Newkirk.

4

Round-the-Clock Protection

At the next corner Nancy made a sharp right and stepped on the accelerator.

"Nancy!" cried Bess, alarmed. "Will you please tell me what's going on? This isn't the way to the police station."

Nancy made another right turn. "I think I just saw Lydia," she said.

"Lydia?" asked Bess, looking surprised. "But she has the flu."

"Well, she must have made a pretty speedy recovery," Nancy said.

Nancy made a last right back onto Center Street and slowed down as she passed the row of stores where she'd just seen the woman in the blue flapper dress. There was no sign of Lydia or anyone else.

"I'm going to park," Nancy said, swallowing her

disappointment, "so we can get a better look." She found a parking spot two blocks farther up the street, and the two girls got out.

"What makes you think it was Lydia you saw?" Bess asked as they walked back down Center Street. "We were going pretty fast."

"I'm not sure it was," Nancy said. "But how many girls do you know in River Heights who'd wear a flapper dress when she's not at a costume party?"

"Maybe it just *looked* like a flapper dress," Bess suggested.

The girls reached the block where Nancy had spotted the young woman, but the only person on the street was an old lady walking a dachshund.

"It looked as if she was in front of an empty store," Nancy said as they passed a deli, a stationer's, and a dry cleaner. "Wait! There it is."

She slowed her pace as they reached a storefront window where a posted sign read, For Rent: Megan Krasnoff Realty, 965 Vernon Road, Call 555-1966.

"I'm sure this was where I saw her," Nancy said excitedly. She peered in through the glass door. There were no lights on inside, but it was easy to see that the store was vacant.

Bess stood next to Nancy and looked through the glass. "You see, Lydia's not there," she said, feeling relieved that her neighbor had not been spotted.

"Or not there *anymore*," Nancy said. Taking her notebook out of her purse, she jotted down the name and number of the real estate company. "I'll follow up on this later," she said. "I don't want to keep Chief McGinnis waiting."

Russell Brown was already sitting in the lobby of the police station when Nancy and Bess arrived. The girls told the desk sergeant that Chief McGinnis was expecting them, then sat down on a bench opposite Brown. Mr. Brown glanced at the girls but didn't seem to recognize them from the day before. He just continued to stare off into space, one foot nervously tapping the floor.

After a moment Chief McGinnis came out to greet them. "Nancy Drew and Bess Marvin," he said, extending his hand. "It's always a mixed blessing to see you. Good, of course, because you make my job easier, but bad because it usually means something's gone wrong in this town."

"Hi, Chief," Nancy said, shaking his hand. Bess did the same.

"And you must be Russell Brown," McGinnis said, turning to the man on the other bench. "These are the girls who found your brooch."

Mr. Brown stood up quickly. "Where is it?" he asked anxiously. "Has it been damaged?"

"Let's go to my office first," Chief McGinnis said. "Come with me."

Russell Brown followed Chief McGinnis and the girls to the police chief's office. Two uniformed officers were standing just inside the door. Nancy recognized Sergeant Rudinsky. To her left was a young man with a ruddy complexion and straight black hair.

"This is Sergeant Margaret Rudinsky and her partner, Joseph Brody, who's just graduated from the police academy. They'll be investigating this case," the chief said as he sat down behind his desk. "Now, let's see what you've got, Nancy."

Nancy removed the handkerchief-wrapped brooch from her purse and delicately lifted back the corners of the cloth.

"You found it!" Officer Brody exclaimed happily. "Case closed. That was easy."

Sergeant Rudinsky's expression did not change, but Nancy saw her eyes move left to look at Brody.

"The case is not quite closed," Chief McGinnis said. "We still have no idea who stole the brooch in the first place. And since the thief wasn't successful, he or she may try again."

Officer Brody blushed and looked down at the floor.

"Is this the brooch?" Chief McGinnis asked Mr. Brown.

Mr. Brown nodded excitedly and reached forward to grab it, but the police chief put his hand out to stop him. "Whoa," he said. "We've got to dust it first for fingerprints." He picked up the phone and pressed some buttons. "McGinnis here," he said. "I want you to send a lab technician up right away."

Within moments a young woman wearing a lab coat and surgical gloves took the brooch and placed it in an evidence bag.

"I want it back quickly," Chief McGinnis told her, "along with the results." After she left, he turned back to the others. "Our best shot at catching the thief is Nancy's clock. For all the thief knows, the brooch is still hidden inside it and hasn't been discovered."

"I see what you're getting at," said Nancy. "We could use the clock as bait to trap the thief. I think whoever stole the brooch is already looking for it." Nancy went on to describe the apparent break-in at Henry Gordon's store.

"What if Mr. Gordon stole it?" Bess pointed out in a quiet voice. "He already knows you have the brooch."

"That's true," Nancy said, looking at Chief McGinnis.

The police chief rubbed his chin thoughtfully. "We'll put a tail on Gordon. That way we'll know if he does anything suspicious."

Nancy nodded. "And if the thief *isn't* Mr. Gordon, he or she probably knows that the clock is mine. There was a card at the expo with my name on it. Also, Henry Gordon must have an invoice for the clock repair in his office that has my name on it. If the thief went to the trouble of breaking into Past Perfect, what's to stop him or her from coming to my house?"

"Exactly," Chief McGinnis said. "And if that happens, we'll be right there waiting. We'll set up a twenty-four-hour surveillance outside your house — plainclothes officers in an unmarked car."

"Hold on a minute," Mr. Brown cut in. "Are you

saying you want to leave my brooch inside her clock instead of giving it back to me?"

"Well, if we give the brooch back to you, the thief would have no way of knowing it," Chief McGinnis said. "He or she might still come after the clock." The police chief sat back in his chair and folded his arms across his chest. "But do you think the brooch will be as safe with you, Mr. Brown, as it would be under constant police protection?"

Over his glasses, Russell Brown eyed the police chief with doubt. "How do I know you and Ms. Drew will keep it safe? I'm sorry. It's just that after what happened yesterday, I'm not feeling too trustful."

"It's quite all right," Chief McGinnis said. "I leave it up to you."

Mr. Brown looked nervously from Nancy to the police chief. "Maybe you're right," he said at last. "I'll let you keep it for now. But *please* guard it with your lives."

Chief McGinnis nodded. "Rudinsky and Brody will take the first shift," he said. "I'll assign other teams to relieve them. Your brooch will be in very good hands."

"I'd like to help in any way I can," Nancy offered. "In addition to keeping the clock, I mean."

"Fine," said the police chief. "I'd be foolish not to take advantage of your detective skills. Just be sure to keep me informed of anything you turn up."

There was a knock on the door. Sergeant Rudinsky

38

opened it, and the lab technician reappeared. "Nothing," she said, placing the brooch on Chief McGinnis's desk. "It's so smudged there's no way of getting a clear print. Sorry."

After the technician left, Chief McGinnis gave the two other officers a nod. "Rudinsky, Brody, change into street clothes and begin the surveillance. You'll be relieved at midnight."

As they all filed out of the police chief's office, Nancy touched Russell Brown on the shoulder. "May I have your business card?" she asked. "I might need to ask you some questions later."

"So far we have more questions than we know what to do with, but not a single answer," Mr. Brown said as he gave her his card.

As Nancy parked in her driveway, she noticed Sergeant Rudinsky and Officer Brody pulling their dark blue unmarked sedan to a halt across the street. They parked between two other cars so they wouldn't be too noticeable.

"Hannah?" Nancy called as she and Bess entered the front door of the Drews' house. There was no answer.

"I'll have to explain about the surveillance later," Nancy said, heading for the study. "But first, I'm going to put the brooch back in Dad's safe. As Chief McGinnis said, the thief will have no way of knowing the brooch isn't still inside the clock."

"Do you have any new ideas about the case?" Bess asked after Nancy had locked the brooch inside the wall safe.

Nancy shook her head. "Our only real suspects so far are Lydia and Henry Gordon, I'm afraid. But I was thinking it would help if we had a list of everyone who attended the expo. Then we could check to see if any other names ring a bell."

"That should be easy to get," said Bess. "We all signed in yesterday, remember? I'm sure that coordinator, the lady in the nice red suit, would have the list. What was her name?"

"Jennings," Nancy said, snapping her fingers. "Mary Lou Jennings. Let's see if she's in the phone book."

The girls went to the kitchen to get the phone book. "Here she is," said Nancy after scanning a page. Within moments, she had called Ms. Jennings and explained what she needed. Nancy was careful not to reveal that the brooch had been located. Ms. Jennings was more than willing to help and invited the girls to come over that afternoon to look at the sign-in lists.

After making themselves some egg salad sandwiches, Nancy and Bess set off for the address Mary Lou Jennings had given Nancy. It was not far from the Drews' home. Nancy turned her sports car up a long, tree-lined driveway that led to a white mansion with columns in front.

"Wow," said Bess in an awed voice. "I'll bet there are at least fifty rooms in this house!"

"Plus one important list of names," Nancy added as they got out of the car.

Mary Lou Jennings opened the door herself when the girls rang the bell. She was dressed more casually than she had been the day before, in a white silk blouse, slim black pants, and flat two-toned pumps. A single wrinkle was etched in her smooth forehead. Behind her, a uniformed maid was dusting a table in the wide entry hall.

"You don't know how upset I am," Ms. Jennings said after Nancy and Bess introduced themselves. "I've organized this event for the past five years, and nothing like this has ever happened before."

Ms. Jennings ushered the girls into a large parlor. "I've set you up in here," she said, showing Nancy and Bess two stapled stacks of paper on a coffee table. "These are the names of all the exhibitors and guests. Make yourselves comfortable, and I'll send Kate in with some cool drinks."

Nancy and Bess thanked Ms. Jennings and went straight to work.

"There are hundreds and hundreds of names," Bess moaned as she flipped through one of the lists. "And we don't even know who we're looking for."

"It's a long shot," Nancy admitted. "Just keep your eyes open for anything that looks interesting."

The maid appeared with lemonade. For half an hour, the girls scanned the lists, pausing only to sip from their tall glasses. After a half hour, Nancy's eyes were tired. She was beginning to get a headache, too.

"Maybe we should—" Nancy started to say, but she was cut off by a yelp from Bess. "What is it?" Nancy asked. "Did you find something?"

"I sure did!" Bess exclaimed. She pointed at her list. "You'll never believe who was at the expo yesterday."

"Who?" Nancy asked. "Tell me!"

"Kimberly Burton," Bess replied in a low, excited voice. "The cat burglar who was in all the papers last year."

5

In the Cat Burglar's Lair

"Kimberly Burton was on the TV news, too," Bess prompted Nancy. "Remember? She was on trial for that string of robberies in River Heights and a couple of other nearby towns."

"I do remember," Nancy said. "And I'm pretty sure I saw her at the expo." She described the woman in black whom she'd noticed when they were about to look at Russell Brown's jewelry. "I thought she looked familiar. That was because I had seen her picture in the newspaper during the trial. I remember it was a really big scandal because she's from a rich local family. But they never convicted her because there wasn't enough evidence."

"The robberies stopped right after the trial, though," Bess pointed out. "That's pretty incriminating, if you ask me."

Just then, Mary Lou Jennings appeared in the doorway. "Have you found something?" she asked. "I hope you don't mind, but I've been hovering right outside. I'm anxious to see this thief captured."

Nancy looked up from the coffee table. "Did you know Kimberly Burton was at the expo?" she asked Ms. Jennings.

A serious expression came over the older woman's face. She came into the room and sat in an armchair facing Nancy and Bess. "I did know that," she said, frowning. "And I know all about the scandal last year. It was particularly painful for me because I know the Burton family quite well. Kimberly's mother and my mother went to school together, and their home is in this neighborhood."

"What can you tell me about Kimberly Burton?" Nancy asked.

The single line reappeared on Ms. Jennings's forehead. "She's a rather unusual person," she said after a short silence. "Kimberly was always getting into trouble, even when she was a little girl. It was always hard to tell, though, whether she was really bad or just wanted everyone to *think* she was. I always believed Kimberly was bored and just wanted to stir up some excitement."

Nancy frowned. "What about the cat burglaries?" Nancy asked. "Do you think she's really a thief?"

"Again, it's hard to say," Ms. Jennings replied with a sigh. "She pleaded not guilty, and the court ruled in her favor. But she *did* seem to enjoy all the publicity surrounding the trial. Some people said she was gloating because she had gotten away with the thefts."

Nancy nodded. "Why do you suppose she was at the expo yesterday?" she asked.

"Why, that's an easy question to answer," said Ms. Jennings. "During the past year, Kimberly's been dealing in antique jewelry. Buying and selling it. I've seen her pieces. They're quite unusual."

"Like the brooch," Bess said under her breath to Nancy. "Maybe the way she acquires her pieces is unusual, too."

"Could be," said Nancy. Turning to Ms. Jennings, she added, "I'd like to speak to Kimberly Burton. Do you know her well enough to arrange an introduction?"

The socialite nodded. "We see each other fairly frequently at auctions."

"I don't want Ms. Burton to know we're investigating the disappearance of the brooch," Nancy said. "Maybe we could tell her we're interested in looking at her jewelry."

"She does have several pieces for sale," Ms. Jennings told Nancy. "Let me see what I can do."

The woman left the parlor and returned a few minutes later. "It's all arranged," she said. "I told Kimberly that you two collect antique jewelry. She said you could come by tomorrow afternoon." Ms.

Jennings handed Nancy a slip of paper. "Here's the address."

The girls thanked Ms. Jennings and got up to leave. Nancy borrowed the lists of names, promising to return them soon.

It was late afternoon when Nancy and Bess returned to the Drews' house, and the girls decided it was too late to go to the lake. The dark blue sedan was still parked across the street, and Hannah still wasn't home. Once inside, Nancy used the kitchen phone to call Chief McGinnis. Bess picked up on the extension in the study to listen.

"It's a good lead," the police chief said when he heard how the girls had spent their afternoon. "But be very careful. Kimberly Burton could be the thief, and that means she might be dangerous."

After they'd hung up, Bess appeared in the kitchen, her blue eyes fearful. "I don't like the way he said that. Do you really think we should go to Kimberly Burton's house without some sort of backup? What if she guesses our real reason for going there?"

"Remember," Nancy said, trying to calm her friend, "the only thing against Kimberly Burton so far is that she was *on trial* for burglary. In this country, a person is innocent until proven guilty. Kimberly Burton was never proven guilty."

Bess didn't seem convinced, but she managed a weak smile.

"If you feel uncomfortable about going with me tomorrow, I'll go by myself," Nancy said.

"Do you think I would give up an opportunity to meet Kimberly Burton?" Bess cried, suddenly herself again. "No way! I couldn't let you go alone."

Nancy smiled. "I'll pick you up at one."

The following afternoon Nancy and Bess drove up another long, tree-lined driveway toward a house that was nearly as large and impressive as Mary Lou Jennings's. This one was a tall stone mansion with towers at the top. Trees surrounding the building cast the house into deep shadow.

"The place looks haunted," Bess remarked as she and Nancy climbed the stone steps to the heavy front door. "Does Kimberly Burton live here all alone?"

Nancy shrugged and rang the doorbell. The girls heard loud chimes echoing inside the house.

A tall, slim woman in her mid-thirties opened the door. Nancy recognized Kimberly Burton immediately from the antiques expo. She was very pretty and dressed entirely in black. Her almond-shaped eyes tilted upward and they were a startling golden yellow.

"She *does* look like a cat, even if she's not a cat burglar," Bess whispered to Nancy.

Nancy hoped the woman hadn't overheard the remark, but she laughed and said, "I see my reputation precedes me. Please call me Kimberly."

To hide her embarrassment, Nancy quickly introduced herself and Bess. "Mary Lou Jennings spoke to you about us yesterday," she added. "We've heard

47

about your antique jewelry collection, and we'd love to see it."

Kimberly smiled slyly without displaying any teeth. "I've been expecting you," she said. "Follow me."

Her dark, slender form retreated silently down a cool, dimly lit passage with walls of gray stone. The house looked even more like a castle inside, Nancy thought. It was decorated with old tapestries and suits of armor. "Wow," Nancy said as the woman led them past a wall completely covered with lances, swords, and daggers. "Those weapons look dangerous."

"I like to live dangerously," Kimberly said. "If you don't take risks, you don't get any rewards."

"Like this beautiful home, I guess," Nancy said, pretending not to notice Kimberly's mysterious tone.

"I wasn't talking about my home," Kimberly told her. "That was acquired through sheer hard work by my grandfather and father, who left it to me. Hard work is not my style, though. I think of work as a game, so it's never hard."

"Is buying and selling jewelry your only business?" Bess asked.

Kimberly smiled and looked meaningfully at Bess. "I have a variety of interests, as you well know."

Bess lowered her eyes, and her face turned bright red. "I'm sorry about what I said before. I know you're not a cat burglar. That remark just slipped out of my mouth."

"How do you know I'm not?" asked Kimberly.

Bess looked confused. Nancy could tell that her

48

friend wasn't sure how to respond to Kimberly's comment.

"I wasn't *convicted*," Kimberly went on. "That doesn't necessarily mean I wasn't guilty." With a graceful movement, she turned and let the girls into a small, dark sitting room.

Kimberly gestured for Nancy and Bess to sit on a carved wooden bench. Next to it was a table covered with red velvet cloth. "I'll be right back," she said.

Nancy waited until she was sure Kimberly was out of hearing range before she spoke. She kept her voice low. "Ms. Jennings was right," she told Bess. "Kimberly Burton is a very unusual character."

"It's almost as if she wants us to think she *was* guilty," Bess whispered.

"If she really was guilty and got away with it, then she has nothing to worry about. She can't be tried again for the same crime," Nancy said.

"I wonder what she's up to," Bess said.

Nancy shrugged. "Beats me."

Several minutes later Kimberly reappeared carrying a wooden tray. When she set it down on the table, Nancy and Bess could see that it held several necklaces, some bracelets, and a large brooch. Kimberly laid them carefully on the red velvet, then stepped back.

The two girls leaned forward to get a closer look. One of the necklaces resembled the one Kimberly was wearing. It was made of squares of hammered silver strung together to form a chain. Another necklace was made of colorful, brightly polished stones with gold beads between them.

Nancy paid particular attention to the brooch. While it didn't look exactly like the rose brooch, it was made in a similar style. It was circular and had been designed to resemble the globe. The continents were mapped in amber and emeralds, and the ocean was made of sapphires. If Kimberly had been drawn to the globe brooch, Nancy thought, she might have been interested in the rose brooch, too—if she'd seen it.

"This is amazing," Nancy said, gently lifting up the heavy brooch.

"Exceptional detail," Bess added. Nancy could tell from the gleam in her friend's eyes that she understood what Nancy was getting at. "I've never seen anything quite like it," Bess added, playing along.

"All my pieces are unique," Kimberly said proudly.

"You mean no one has used precious stones this way before?" Nancy asked in her most innocent-sounding voice.

Kimberly raised one eyebrow and looked down at her. Nancy couldn't tell if her expression was one of guilt, surprise, or annoyance.

"This piece has not been duplicated," Kimberly said.

Nancy tried not to groan. Kimberly's answers weren't getting them anywhere.

"And where did you get this one?" Bess asked.

"I never reveal my sources," replied Kimberly.

"Trade secrets, you know. So tell me, do any of these pieces interest you?"

"I'm interested in the brooch," Nancy told her. "How much does it cost?"

"Thirty thousand dollars," said Kimberly.

Nancy used every ounce of her self-control not to flinch. She knew she'd burst out laughing if she looked at Bess, so she stared down at the brooch. "I see," she said, trying to sound as if she spent that kind of money on jewelry all the time. "I'll need time to think about it."

"Of course," Kimberly replied smoothly.

"Could we come back to look at it again?" Nancy asked.

"Of course," the woman said. "I'll look forward to our next meeting." She flashed her catlike smile again. "Shall I show you out?"

Kimberly Burton led the girls back to the front hall and waved as they walked down the stone steps. Then she shut the heavy wooden door.

"She's really puzzling," Bess said, shivering even though it was eighty degrees outside. "I mean, I don't know how to take anything she says. Is she serious, or making fun of us, or what?"

Nancy shook her head as she unlocked the car door, and she and Bess got in. "That's what we'll have to find out, I guess."

Nancy turned the key to start the car, but nothing happened. "That's funny," she said.

"Are we out of gas?" Bess asked.

Nancy shook her head. "I filled the tank this morning. Let me check under the hood." She popped the hood lever, then got out of the car.

"Nan?" Bess called through the window when Nancy didn't come back right away. "Is there a problem?"

"I think you'd better come here," came Nancy's voice from behind the hood.

When Bess got to the front of the car, she gasped in dismay. Every visible wire and hose had been slashed, and the battery was gone.

"I also found this," Nancy said, holding out a small piece of paper. It read: The clock is ticking, but not for long. Time's up, Nancy Drew!

6

Over the Edge

Bess began to shake again, and her eyes were wide with fear as she looked at Nancy. "'T-time's up'? I don't like the sound of that."

Nancy put an arm around her friend's shoulders. "It might not be as bad as you think," she said, trying to look on the bright side. "It could just mean the thief has finally figured out that the clock belongs to me, and he's going to come after it. That's what we've been waiting for, right?"

"That's only one possible meaning of 'time's up,'" Bess said, "and I don't like the other one. Who knows how far the thief will go to get the brooch back? Look what he's done already!" Bess pointed to the sliced wires under Nancy's hood. "He must have had a really sharp knife."

"Or she," Nancy reminded her, thinking of

Kimberly Burton's collection of medieval weapons. "We may have walked right into the thief's arms . . . or house."

Bess's eyes widened. "Do you think Kimberly did this?" she asked.

"I'm not sure," Nancy replied. "But here's one theory. Kimberly was at the expo. She steals the brooch and hides it inside the clock, but she can't get it out without being caught by the police. Then the clock gets packed up, and she has to figure out where it went. First she tries Mr. Gordon's store. She doesn't find it there, but maybe she finds the card or some piece of paper saying the clock is mine. She plans to track me down, but instead, we come right to her."

"But of course she can't just ask you for the brooch," Bess said, picking up on Nancy's reasoning. "So she sneaks outside, trashes your car, and leaves the note to scare you." Bess thought for a moment. "She *was* gone a pretty long time when she went to get the jewelry."

"Exactly," Nancy agreed. "The other possibility is that we were followed here. The thief—whether it's Lydia or someone else—could have followed me here."

"But Lydia already knows where you live," Bess said. "She wouldn't have to come all the way out here to do this to your car. And she wouldn't have had to go to all that trouble to find out who owned the clock."

"Unless she wanted to make it look as if someone else did it," Nancy pointed out. "As I said before, she could have made it *look* like a break-in at Mr. Gordon's store. But no matter who the thief is, I have a feeling he or she will come after the clock soon—maybe tonight."

"So now what do we do?" Bess asked. "We're stuck here without transportation. We certainly can't go back into Kimberly's house to ask for help."

"Sure we can," Nancy said. "In fact, that's exactly what we're going to do."

"Are you kidding?" Bess asked in alarm. "Who knows what she could do to us in that scary old house? Maybe she has ancient torture equipment down in the dungeon."

"Whether she does or not," Nancy said, "she's not going to do a thing to us."

Bess shot Nancy a wary glance. "How can you be so sure?"

"She's far too clever to be so obvious," Nancy said, heading for the stone steps. "Whether she's innocent or guilty, she'll at least let us use her phone."

"I'll tell you what," Bess said, opening the door to Nancy's car. "I'll stay here. If you don't come out in five minutes, I'll run and get help."

"Okay," Nancy said with a laugh. "But I'm sure you won't have to do anything so drastic." She walked back to the mansion, rang the doorbell, and again heard the deep chimes echoing through the house.

Kimberly opened the door and smiled at Nancy. "Back so soon?" she asked. "I didn't know you felt so strongly about the brooch."

Nancy studied Kimberly, wondering if her words had a double meaning. Which brooch was she talking about?

Nancy explained what had happened to her car and asked to use the phone.

Kimberly frowned and lowered her eyebrows, but she showed no other reaction to Nancy's predicament. "I didn't realize I lived in such a dangerous neighborhood," she said. "You can use the phone in the hall."

She led Nancy to an alcove off the entrance hall. There, on a dark wooden table, was an old-fashioned black dial phone. When Nancy picked up the heavy receiver, she noticed that Kimberly moved away but stayed close enough to hear.

First, Nancy called information for the number of a towing company and arranged to have her car picked up. Next, she called home to see if Hannah could come and get her and Bess, but there was no answer. Nancy didn't want to bother her father at the office. She was beginning to think she and Bess would have to make the long way home on foot when she suddenly remembered George's mobile phone.

Taking her wallet out of her purse, she rummaged through it and finally found George's number. Nancy dialed and waited through several rings before she heard her friend's familiar voice.

"George!" Nancy cried. "I'm so happy you're there."

"Nancy?" George's voice sounded far away. "Hold on a second."

More faintly, Nancy heard her asking someone whether he wanted rainbow or chocolate sprinkles. Then George was back on the line. "Sorry," she said. "What's going on?"

Nancy explained the situation. "Do you think you could come and get us?" she asked. "Is it out of your way?"

"You're in luck," said George. "When I'm done in this neighborhood, I'll be heading that way. Give me the address. I should be there in about half an hour."

"Terrific! Thanks, George." Nancy gave her directions and hung up.

"You're more than welcome to wait indoors," Kimberly offered.

Though Nancy didn't believe Bess's fears about Kimberly's "dungeon," she knew she'd feel safer outside, since Kimberly might have been the one who damaged her car. "Thanks," she said. "But my friend will be here any minute."

Shortly after a tow truck had carted Nancy's blue sports car away, Nancy and Bess heard a happy, tinkling tune in the distance. Gradually it grew louder and louder until a square white Frosty Freeze truck turned into Kimberly Burton's long driveway.

"George!" Bess called, running toward her cousin as the truck came to a stop.

George hopped out of the truck and onto the driveway, wearing her white Frosty Freeze smock and cap. She was grinning and holding out two paper-wrapped Popsicles. "Try a Rocket Pop," she said.

"Don't mind if I do," Bess said. "All this waiting in the hot sun has made me thirsty."

Nancy took the other Popsicle. "You're a lifesaver, George."

"No problem," said George. "Hop in. There's only one passenger seat, but I think you'll both fit."

"I don't know about that, after all the ice cream you've been feeding me," Bess said.

Nancy and Bess squeezed into the front seat and fastened the seat belt around both of them as George set the truck in motion and drove back out to the street. "I hope you don't mind if I can't take you home right away. I've got another hour left on my shift. Then I have to take the truck back to headquarters. It's only a few exits away on the highway."

"Don't mind us," Nancy said, licking her Rocket Pop. "But do you think we could make a short stop before you leave River Heights? It should only take a minute."

George shrugged. "Sure. Meanwhile, it's time to make the little kiddies happy." She pressed a button on the dashboard, and the cheerful song blared out of the speaker on top of the truck.

Bess stopped eating her Rocket Pop for a moment to listen. "That's such a cute song," she said.

* * *

"Don't you ever get sick of that song?" Bess asked an hour later as the Frosty Freeze truck pulled away from its last stop. "I mean, the same thing over and over and over again." She covered her ears with her hands. "It's awful!"

"You stop hearing it after a while," George said, laughing at her cousin. "Where to, Nan?"

Nancy checked her notebook. "Megan Krasnoff Realty, nine sixty-five Vernon Road," she said. "That's between Center and Grove streets."

On the way, Nancy and Bess filled George in on Lydia's mysterious appearance at the vacant store, as well as their visits to Mary Lou Jennings and Kimberly Burton.

"I want to know if it really was Lydia I saw," Nancy said as they pulled up in front of the real estate office. "And if it was, we need to find out what she was doing there. I'll be right back."

Megan Krasnoff Realty was located in a small brick building on a residential street. The door was open, so Nancy walked in. A young man with slicked-back hair was sitting behind the nearest desk.

"May I help you?" he asked, looking up at Nancy.

Nancy improvised quickly. "I saw your For Rent sign in that vacant store on Center Street, the one next to the dry cleaner. I was wondering if it was still available."

"I'll have to check," the man said. He tapped a few keys on his computer keyboard. Nancy tried discreetly to move behind him so she could see what information came up on the monitor, but the man blocked her view.

"I'm sorry," he said after a moment. "It's already been rented. Perhaps I could show you something else? We have several properties on Main Street, which is a good location for a business."

"No," Nancy told him. "I really had my heart set on Center Street. You wouldn't happen to know who rented it?"

The young man gave her an apologetic look. "We can't give out that information."

"Oh," Nancy said, disappointed. Then she had an idea. Pretending she needed something in her pocketbook, she set it down on the corner of his desk, then let it drop to the floor. "I'm so sorry," she said as the man leaned over to pick up her purse.

As soon as he bent forward, Nancy looked at the monitor. The print was small, but she could see one thing clearly. The person who'd rented the property was Lydia Newkirk.

Nancy took the purse from the man and said, "Please forgive me. Sometimes I can be so clumsy."

"No trouble," he told her. "You're sure there isn't any other neighborhood you'd consider? We have lots of listings right now."

"Let me think about it," Nancy said. "I'll call you." She slung her purse over her shoulder and headed for the door.

"I don't believe it," Bess said, after Nancy told her

and George what she'd found out in the office. "I've never known Lydia to be a liar."

"Facts are facts," said George as she pulled away. "First she lied about having the flu, and now she's sneaking around behind her boss's back."

"And if she's planning to start a business," Nancy added, "she needs a lot of cash. What better way to get it than to sell an expensive piece of jewelry?"

"Sounds like a definite motive to me," George agreed.

"So now we have two very strong suspects," Nancy said. "Kimberly Burton and Lydia. Mr. Gordon's still on the list, too, but so far nothing points to him. I spoke to Chief McGinnis this morning. He said Mr. Gordon hasn't done anything except go to work and then return home at night."

"This is such a pretty drive," Nancy said as they followed the road's graceful curves. On either side of the highway were gently sloping hills with thick green foliage. As they neared the steep gorge that gave River Heights its name, the hills became rockier and there were fewer trees. The highway led onto the River Heights Bridge, which crossed the Muskoka River.

As they neared the bridge, George swerved sharply into the right lane.

"Why'd you do that?" Nancy asked, holding on to the passenger door to keep from lurching into Bess.

George pressed her lips together and glanced at the rearview mirror.

"George? Is something wrong?" Nancy asked.

"I don't know," said George, looking at the mirror again. "But I have a feeling we're being followed."

Turning around in her seat, Nancy saw an orange van driving close behind the Frosty Freeze truck.

"Switch lanes again," she told George. "Let's see what they do."

George quickly moved back into the left lane. The orange van did the same.

"Oh, great," said Bess. "This has been one terrific day." Her tone was sarcastic, but Nancy thought she saw a hint of fear in her friend's eyes.

Suddenly the orange van moved closer and bumped the Frosty Freeze truck from behind.

"George!" Bess said nervously. She braced herself against the dashboard and turned around to look at the van. "Can you shake them?"

"I'm going to try," George said, fighting to keep the truck from swerving. "But this truck wasn't exactly built for speed." She jammed her foot on the accelerator and moved back into the right lane. The orange van sped up also and pulled up alongside them.

Nancy turned her head to get a better look at the van. It was painted orange all over except for three narrow lime-green stripes running along the side. The windows were tinted, so she couldn't see who was inside, and she couldn't get a look at the license plate.

"Can you go any faster?" Nancy asked George.

George shook her head grimly. "I've already got my foot all the way to the floor."

Just then the van started to bump their left side. George tried valiantly to outmaneuver the van, but still it kept bumping them, pushing them closer and closer to the bridge railing.

"Oh, no!" Bess cried, gripping the dash so tightly that her knuckles turned white. "We're going to go over!"

Nancy tried not to let herself look to the right at the steel railing, the only thing that stood between them and a steep drop into the river below. "Don't worry. The guardrail will hold," she said, trying to sound convincing.

The orange van gave another shove, stronger than the first. George clung desperately to the wheel, turning it sharply to the left. But the van's impact was too powerful. It forced the Frosty Freeze truck right through the bridge's metal guardrail.

7

A Valuable Discovery

Nancy, Bess, and George screamed as the Frosty Freeze truck tore through the metal rail with a loud screech. The impact caused them to lurch forward against their seat belts.

When the girls looked up, they saw that the truck was teetering precariously over the side of the bridge, still tinkling its happy tune. Like a giant seesaw, it tipped forward, caught on its rear axle. Nancy could see the rushing waters of the Muskoka River far below.

"What are we going to do?" Bess wailed. Then, trying to get control of herself, she smiled weakly. "Maybe we'll get to go swimming after all."

"We won't be swimming," George said. "We'll be driftwood. If we fall, the force of the impact will kill us!"

Suddenly Nancy had an idea.

"George, is there a back door to this truck?" When George nodded, Nancy unhooked the safety belt she and Bess shared. "We've got to move—*now!*" she said in an urgent voice.

Quickly undoing her own seat belt, George grabbed her mobile phone, and all three girls scrambled toward the back of the truck. George struggled with the latch on the door.

"Hurry!" Bess urged, her voice trembling.

Finally George got the latch open, and Nancy gave the door a powerful kick.

"Jump!" Nancy cried as the door flew open.

All three girls landed in a pile on the pavement. Quickly untangling themselves, they stood up in a daze. Traffic had stopped in both directions, and several motorists rushed over to see if the girls were all right. The orange van was nowhere in sight.

"I'll call the police," George said, pulling her phone out of its pouch.

Bess glanced back at the truck, which was still hanging over the water. Suddenly she burst into tears. "Oh, Nancy, I really thought we were going to . . ."

"But we didn't," said Nancy, giving her friend a hug. "We got out in time."

"This time," Bess said through her tears. "But who knows when our luck will run out?"

Within minutes a police car pulled up, and two officers jumped out. One, a tall, heavyset man, took a look at the ice cream truck, then ran to the trunk of the police car and removed a coil of heavy cable. He threw it to his partner, a petite blond woman.

"Secure it to the post," said the officer, whose nameplate read Robert Walker. "I'll radio for a tow truck."

Nancy turned to Bess and George. "We sure are giving the towing companies a lot of business today."

The blond officer, whose name was Jean Daniel, attached the cable to a hitch on the back of the ice cream truck. Then she looped the other end several times around a steel post on the bridge and secured it.

Officer Walker spoke into his walkie-talkie and then turned to the girls. "Looks like you had a little problem here."

Nancy explained how they'd nearly been run off the road, giving the policeman a detailed description of the van.

"An orange van with green stripes," Officer Walker mumbled, jotting down the information Nancy had given him. "No license plate number?"

Nancy shook her head. "I tried, but we just couldn't get a good look."

"I see," said Officer Walker. "We'll run a check and see what we come up with."

"When you talk to Chief McGinnis," Nancy added, "please mention that this incident was probably related to the stolen brooch."

For the second time that day a tow truck appeared, dodging in and out of the stalled traffic on the bridge. The driver got out and, aided by Officer Walker, placed an enormous metal hook underneath the back of the Frosty Freeze truck. After Officer Daniel removed the cable, the tow truck slowly pulled the ice cream truck back onto the bridge. The motorists standing nearby applauded.

Nancy, Bess, and George walked around the Frosty Freeze truck to assess the damage. The front fender and hood were dented where they had struck the railing, and the headlights were shattered. When George turned the ignition key she was relieved to hear that the engine was still running smoothly and that the merry tune still played, as well.

"What should I do with the truck?" the tow truck driver asked. "You want me to take it somewhere?"

George shook her head. "No, thanks. As long as I can still drive it, I'm going to take it back myself. It would look much worse if my boss saw it hanging off a tow truck."

"Just as long as your boss sees this," the truck driver said, handing George a bill.

George grimaced. "I'm a little nervous about showing this to Ms. Franklin, my supervisor," she said to Nancy and Bess.

"And I'm a lot nervous about getting back into that truck," Bess added, her blue eyes lingering on the truck's dented front end. "Maybe the police officers can give us a ride home."

"The damage has already been done," Nancy said. "I doubt the van's going to come back for us. They probably think we're floating in the river by now."

"Who would do such a thing?" Bess wondered. "Okay, I'll go." Turning to her cousin, she added, "Just do me one favor."

"Sure," agreed George. "Name it."

"Turn off that stupid music!"

Laughing, George did as Bess had asked. Then, after thanking the police officers for their help, the three girls climbed into the Frosty Freeze truck and took off.

As they drove, Nancy took her notebook from her purse and flipped it open. "The driver of that van could have been anybody," she said, looking at the notes she had taken on the case so far. "Lydia, Kimberly Burton, or some person we haven't encountered yet."

"Those wild colors on the van would certainly fit Lydia's personality," George commented.

"Kimberly's, too," said Bess. "And since Kimberly's an antiques dealer, she probably needs a van."

"For jewelry?" Nancy asked.

"We don't know what else she deals in," Bess reminded her. "She said she has a variety of interests, whatever that means."

"That's true," Nancy said. "Maybe Chief McGinnis can run a check on Lydia and Kimberly to see what kind of cars are registered in their names. But I keep thinking about the possibility of another suspect. I have a weird feeling about that van, as if I've seen it somewhere before. But not with Lydia or Kimberly in it. I would have remembered that."

George's brow was knit in concentration. "You know, I think I've seen that van before, too. Only I can't remember where."

"It's also possible that the driver of the van is working with either Lydia or Kimberly," Nancy pointed out. At the bottom of her list of suspects, she added a big question mark.

George turned off the highway and onto a private road that went up a hill. Soon they reached a small guard's house and an electronic gate. George flashed her Frosty Freeze ID card at the guard, and the gate slowly opened.

"Wow," Bess said. "Tight security. Are they afraid someone's going to hijack an ice cream truck?"

"It's company policy," George said. "Every employee has to have an ID card."

George drove into an enormous parking lot filled with Frosty Freeze trucks and employees' cars. Several large buildings were clustered together next to the lot. Nancy saw a few smaller buildings at the other end of the parking area. Pulling in between two other trucks, George parked, and the girls got out.

"Do you want us to come with you for moral support?" Nancy asked.

"Yeah, we can back up your story," Bess offered.

George shook her head. "Ms. Franklin's pretty fair, and I've got the police report to prove I'm telling the truth. I'll be back in a couple of minutes." George took a few steps away, then looked back at them over her shoulder. "Of course, if I *do* lose my job, I'll have

69

more time to help you with the case . . . and my car's still running."

"Good luck," Nancy said, and Bess gave her cousin the thumbs-up sign.

Ten minutes later George rejoined them in the parking lot, a big smile on her face.

"You're still employed?" Bess asked hopefully.

George nodded. "Ms. Franklin was really understanding. She said the company's insurance would cover the damage. She blamed me for only one thing."

"What's that?" asked Nancy.

"Transporting unauthorized parties in a company vehicle."

"I think she means us," Bess said to Nancy.

George nodded. "But I can still help out with transportation. I'm not working tomorrow, so I can drive you around. And the day after, you can use my car, as long as you drive me here for work."

"Thanks, George," Nancy said. "That would be a big help." She and Bess followed George to her car.

"Would you mind making one more stop?" Nancy asked as they pulled out of the Frosty Freeze parking lot. "I just realized we're not far from Russell Brown's shop. It's on Route Twenty-two, on the other side of the bridge."

"No problem," George said.

"Oh, no!" cried Bess. "We have to go over that bridge again?"

"There's no other way to get there," Nancy said.

"I'll cover my eyes," Bess said. "Just tell me when we're back on solid ground."

Several minutes later George pulled her car over to the side of a country road and parked next to a wooden sign that had the words Russell Brown Antiques painted on it in faded white letters. A path led from the sign to a red farmhouse with white trim.

Bells jingled as Nancy opened the door and entered the house, Bess and George behind her. Russell Brown was standing inside.

"May I help . . ." he began, but then he recognized Nancy and Bess. "Oh," he said. "It's you. Have you had any progress catching the thief?"

"Not yet," Nancy told him. She introduced George to the store owner, then looked around. Mr. Brown had converted most of the ground floor of the house to the antique shop. Most of the pieces looked right at home in the old farmhouse. There were patchwork quilts and hand-painted wooden cabinets and even an old rocking horse. Nancy liked the homey, comfortable appearance of the rooms.

"Have you come to look at my collection?" Mr. Brown asked.

Nancy turned to face him. "No," she said. "But I'd like to ask you a few questions."

"More questions," Mr. Brown said with a wry grin.

"I'm sorry," Nancy said. "This won't take long. Can you tell me where you got the brooch? We really don't know that much about it."

Mr. Brown waved a hand toward the back of the house. "Do you know how many pieces pass through here every week?" he asked. "I couldn't possibly remember where I got each and every one."

"Well, you must keep some sort of record," Nancy pressed. "Could you possibly look it up? It might be an important clue."

Mr. Brown walked to the back of the room and opened a wooden filing cabinet. "I remember that the brooch belonged to an elderly woman," he mumbled as he riffled through the files. Finally he pulled out a manila folder. "Here it is. According to this, it belonged to a woman named Agnes Thompson. She died several months before the piece was brought to me."

"When was that?" Nancy asked.

"A few months back," Mr. Brown said vaguely. "I don't remember exactly."

"And that's all you can tell us?" Nancy asked.

Brown shrugged. "Where I get a piece is not as important to me as selling it."

There was a jingling of bells, and a young man and woman entered. They wore business suits and carried matching briefcases.

"Now if you'll excuse me," Mr. Brown said. He rushed past Nancy to greet the couple. "May I help you?"

Mr. Brown followed closely behind the pair as they wandered around the store.

"He's not very helpful, is he?" Bess whispered to

Nancy, then said, "These prices are just as outrageous as the ones we saw at the expo."

George shook her head. "I bet he doesn't do much business with his things costing this much."

Seeing that Mr. Brown was occupied, Nancy put her plan into motion. "Wait here," she told Bess and George in a low voice. "I'll be right back."

She had noticed that Mr. Brown had left the folder open on his desk. Pretending to be interested in a rocking chair right next to the desk, Nancy walked across the room.

When Mr. Brown followed the couple behind a tall dresser, Nancy shifted her gaze to the folder. It lay open, revealing several sheets of paper. Nancy didn't dare risk moving the papers, so she took in as much as she could see. A paper beneath the top one stuck out a little on one side, and Nancy saw the name Thompson written on it.

Then she took a closer look at the paper on top. When she saw what it was, she was barely able to suppress her excitement.

It was a fifty-thousand-dollar insurance policy for the rose brooch. That wasn't so strange—Mr. Brown had said it was worth that much. What interested Nancy more was the date typed at the top of the page. It wasn't from a few months ago, when Mr. Brown had said he got the brooch. It was dated just a few days before the antiques expo.

That seemed a little *too* coincidental. If the brooch

is so valuable, Nancy thought, why would Mr. Brown wait until right before the expo to insure it . . . unless he *knew* it was going to be stolen? He could collect fifty thousand dollars if someone took the brooch. Maybe Russell Brown had arranged the robbery himself!

8

Break-in!

Nancy walked casually back to Bess and George. "Let's go," she said in an excited whisper, giving her friends a look that said she would explain once they were outside.

"Thanks, Mr. Brown," Nancy called, opening the door.

The antique dealer turned around as the three girls left. "Let me know if you come up with anything, Nancy," he called to her.

Once outside, Nancy didn't head for the car but walked toward the back of the building.

"Where are you going?" George asked.

Nancy put a finger to her lips. "I'm looking for an orange van," she whispered.

Bess gasped. "You think it was Mr. Brown?" she asked.

"I'll tell you in the car," Nancy said.

While Bess and George went down the path to the car, Nancy circled the farmhouse, looking for a garage, a clump of trees, or anything else that might conceal a van. There was nothing except flat, dry ground and a gray sedan parked in the driveway. Disappointed, Nancy followed the drive to the road and got into the back seat of George's car.

"What did you find?" George asked, turning around in the driver's seat to look at Nancy.

"Not a van," Nancy admitted, "but you'll never believe what was on Brown's desk." She described the insurance policy.

"You mean he *wanted* the brooch stolen?" Bess asked.

"Very possibly," Nancy replied, "though I'm still not ruling out a real robbery."

"What about the orange van?" George asked.

Nancy sighed. "It's not parked here. But Brown could have hidden it somewhere else. It's also possible that he's working with whoever was driving the van."

"So now we have three definite suspects and a question mark," George said.

"Exactly," said Nancy with a nod. She opened her notebook and added Russell Brown's name to her list. "Brown could be working with Lydia or Kimberly, or with someone else. If only I could remember where I saw that orange van before. . . ."

"I've been thinking about that, too," George said.

"I have the impression I've seen more than one of them. And remember those green stripes along the side? I keep thinking they're a logo for a company or something."

Nancy nodded. "Right. This is going to bother me until we figure it out."

George started the car and drove to Nancy's house to drop her off. "So what's the plan for tomorrow?" she asked.

Nancy leaned forward over the front seat. "I think it's time we paid Lydia a visit. And I'd like to spend some time tracking down the orange van. But in all the excitement today, we've forgotten the main thing."

"I haven't forgotten," Bess said, grimacing. "'The clock is ticking, but not for long.'"

"Right," Nancy said. "Tonight could be the night."

George looked a little worried. "You'll call us if there's any trouble, right?"

"Thanks for the support," Nancy said, "but there are two police officers sitting in an unmarked car right across the street." She nodded toward the dark blue sedan. "Speaking of which, I'm going to check and see how they're doing. Thanks for the ride."

"Good luck tonight, Nancy," Bess called as Nancy got out of the car.

Nancy waved as George's car took off. Checking first to see that no one was watching, she crossed the street and approached the unmarked police car.

Sergeant Rudinsky, bleary-eyed and wearing Bermuda shorts and a tank top, sat behind the wheel. Next to her, Officer Brody sat sipping coffee out of a paper cup.

The sergeant's head jerked up when she saw Nancy. "Oh, it's you," she said, relieved.

"I was just wondering if you'd seen anything," Nancy said.

Sergeant Rudinsky grabbed her notebook off the front seat and read from it quickly. "At four forty-seven P.M., a Caucasian female, late sixties, gray hair, no visible scars or birthmarks, pulled up in a late-model station wagon with bags of groceries. Since the female had keys to the house, we assumed she was a resident."

Nancy laughed. "That was Hannah, our house-keeper."

Suddenly Officer Brody threw himself across the front seat and waved Nancy away from the car. "Someone's coming!" he cried.

Startled, Nancy turned as a second car pulled into her driveway and a man in his forties got out. "That's my dad," she said, laughing. "I assure you he's authorized to enter the house. So when is your shift over?"

"Midnight," answered Sergeant Rudinsky. "Then Walker and Daniel take over. They're a good team."

"I know," Nancy said, remembering the efficient officers who'd helped her on the bridge earlier that afternoon.

Officer Brody looked at Nancy with curiosity. "You sure seem to know a lot about the police department."

Nancy tried to explain. "I've lived in River Heights a long time," she told Officer Brody. "Detective work is a hobby of mine." Then she turned to leave. "Thanks for your help," she added, and went into her house.

As Nancy set the table for dinner she explained to her father and Hannah why the police officers were guarding the house.

"Here we go again," Hannah said as she tossed the pasta salad. "Nancy, after all your cases, I still don't know whether you go looking for trouble or it finds you. You're telling me we're supposed to sit in the house and wait for someone to break in?"

Carson Drew sat down at one end of the dining room table and helped himself to a piece of chicken. "I don't feel too comfortable about this, either," he said to his daughter.

Nancy put down a basket of rolls. "The police are right outside," she said. "They'll probably spot the intruder before we do. But just in case, we can call 911, and the station will radio the officers. We'll be protected either way."

"Why don't I feel reassured?" Hannah asked, shaking her head.

Nancy looked back and forth from Hannah to her father. They were both worried about the case already, so Nancy decided not to tell them about the accident on the River Heights Bridge. Besides, every-thing had turned out all right.

"It's a good thing the brooch is in the safe," said Carson, "in case the thief *does* manage to steal the clock."

Hannah frowned. "I'd just as soon have the clock out of the house," she said. "It started you off in this detective business, and ever since, you've been in one dangerous situation after another."

"We always end up okay," Nancy said, giving the housekeeper a warm smile.

"So far, but who knows if your luck will run out?"

Without thinking, Nancy said, "That's funny. Bess said the same thing today." Then she remembered Bess had been talking about the bridge incident, the one she hadn't mentioned to her father and Hannah, and Nancy fell suddenly silent.

"What are you talking about?" Hannah asked with alarm.

"Er, nothing," Nancy said, pushing her plate away. "I'm going up to my room to wait."

Hannah looked at Nancy's plate. "You haven't touched your chicken."

"I'll tell you what," Nancy said. "I'll take my plate up to my room and nibble tonight while I'm waiting."

Hannah sighed. "If you get hungry later, there's a fresh-baked chocolate cake in the refrigerator. I made it from scratch."

"Mmmm, my favorite." Nancy rose from her chair and picked up her plate with one hand. With the other, she gave Hannah a squeeze. "You're the greatest, Hannah," she said. Then she blew her father a kiss. "And you're not so bad, either."

Plate in hand, Nancy took the stairs to her room two steps at a time. She put the plate on her desk and glanced at the old clock on her dresser. The clock, now running smoothly, showed that the time was seven-fifteen. The wait would probably be several hours at least. Nancy flipped open her pad and studied her notes. She hoped her mind would make some connection it hadn't before, but there were still so many missing pieces.

Sometime later Nancy raised her head from the desk and rubbed her eyes. She must have dozed off. After all she'd been through that day, it wasn't surprising. Nancy looked at the mantel clock and saw that it was ten. She should get ready for bed or at least make it look as if she were asleep.

Without changing out of her jeans and T-shirt, Nancy got into bed, pulled the sheet over her, and turned out the light. The thief wasn't going to break in if he or she thought someone in the house was still awake.

Nancy awoke again, suddenly, thinking she'd heard a loud noise. She wasn't sure whether she'd actually heard the sound or just dreamed it. Sitting up slowly in her bed, she listened carefully. The only sound was the crickets chirping outside her window.

Then she heard it again. A bumping sound, as if someone had tripped over a piece of furniture downstairs. The thief had broken in! Not daring to turn on her light, Nancy fumbled in the dark for her phone.

She had just managed to grab the phone cord when she heard the sound of footsteps creaking on the stairs. Where were the police? Nancy thought frantically. Hadn't they noticed the break-in? The footsteps grew louder and nearer. Nancy could hear her heart pounding in her chest. The thief was heading right for her room!

9

Midnight Getaway

Hoping it wasn't too late, Nancy pulled the push-button phone toward her. She lifted the receiver as quietly as she could, grateful that she'd chosen a model with glow-in-the-dark numbers. Hurriedly she pressed 911 and waited, her heart still pounding.

"Emergency assistance, may I help you?" said a loud male voice.

Nancy heard another creak on the staircase. The thief was getting closer.

"Hello," she whispered. "This is Nancy Drew in River Heights. Someone has broken into my house."

"Emergency assistance," the voice repeated. "Is anyone there?"

He couldn't hear her, but Nancy was afraid to speak any louder.

Officer Brody wasn't, however. At that moment, his voice came blaring over a loudspeaker outside. "We know you're in there," he called. "The house is surrounded. Come out with your hands up."

Nancy heard the footsteps retreat quickly down the stairs, followed by another thud as the intruder hit a piece of furniture. There was silence. Nancy replaced the receiver in its cradle and waited. Since she didn't know whether the thief was still inside the house, she didn't dare leave her room. He or she might have a weapon.

After several minutes, Nancy couldn't bear to keep still any longer. Creeping toward her bedroom door, she slowly turned the knob and pulled the door open a few inches. Her eyes, already used to the dark, made out the shadowy stairway. A shaft of moonlight, shining through the dining room window, made a diagonal stripe across the front hall floor. What was happening? Where was the thief?

Suddenly Officer Brody's voice broke the stillness again. "Stop or I'll shoot!" he warned.

Sergeant Rudinsky must have grabbed the microphone, because her voice now rang out loud and clear. "You are in violation of the U.S. Penal Code for criminal trespassing, breaking and entering, attempted robbery, and resisting arrest. If you don't stop right now, you'll just make it worse for yourself."

Nancy jumped as a gunshot shattered the night.

Then the whole house sprang to life. Nancy saw Hannah's bedroom light come on, immediately followed by Carson's. Fully dressed, the housekeeper and Nancy's father ran into the upstairs hall, where Nancy was already standing.

"I heard the footsteps," Hannah said anxiously. "Do you think they caught him?"

"There's only one way to find out," Nancy said, leading the way down the stairs.

"Don't go outside," her father warned. "There could be more shooting."

Nancy rushed to the dining-room window and peered out into the street, followed by her father and Hannah. By the light of the moon and the streetlights, they could see the police officers in front of their car. But there was no intruder in handcuffs.

Going to the front of the house, Carson Drew opened the door. "Is it safe to come out?" he called.

"Don't worry," Sergeant Rudinsky yelled back. "The intruder left the area. It's safe to come out now."

"What happened?" Nancy asked, as she, her father, and Hannah joined the officers.

"It's more like what *didn't* happen," the sergeant muttered. Officer Brody looked crushed, and his partner turned to Nancy. "We saw the suspect approach the house from the back. He entered the house by way of a side window. If my partner hadn't spoken so soon, we might have trapped him inside."

Sergeant Rudinsky faced Brody. "Why did you say that the house was surrounded?" she asked. "We hadn't even radioed for backup yet."

"I thought if we scared him, he'd be too afraid to come out," Officer Brody said, looking down at the ground.

"Not only were you mistaken," the sergeant told him, "but you also violated procedure."

"Wait a minute," Nancy said to Officer Brody. "You said 'him.' Does that mean you at least got a look at the suspect? Was it a man?"

"We don't know," Sergeant Rudinsky answered briskly. "Those bushes near the house made it difficult to see the suspect clearly. It could have been a woman."

Nancy sighed in frustration. After all the trouble they'd gone to, they didn't know anything more than they had before.

The sound of engines caused Nancy to turn. Two police cars were cruising slowly up the street, their headlights out. They stopped half a block away, and several dark figures emerged from each car.

As the figures approached, Nancy recognized Chief McGinnis's familiar silhouette. When she waved, the police chief hesitated. Sergeant Rudinsky, also spotting the chief, gave him a hand signal, and the chief came forward.

"He got away?" Chief McGinnis asked as he and the other officers rushed forward. Nancy recognized Officers Walker and Daniel among them.

Sergeant Rudinsky nodded.

"How did this happen?" the police chief asked.

Nancy saw Officer Brody glance nervously toward

his partner. He was probably waiting to see if she would reveal his mistake.

"There was a lot of confusion," Sergeant Rudinsky said, "and it was dark near the house. The thief managed to get away before we could stop him . . . or her."

Officer Brody gave his partner a grateful look.

"Did the thief get the brooch?" the police chief asked.

"No," Nancy answered. "The thief never even got near the clock. The brooch is inside my dad's safe."

"Good. That means we have another chance," Chief McGinnis said. "But we're going to have to play it differently this time."

Nancy looked at the police chief. "You mean, since the thief didn't get what he came for, he'll probably try again."

"Yes," replied Chief McGinnis. "But only if it looks as if we've called off the surveillance." He thought for a moment. "Maybe we should have done this in the first place."

"Done what?" Nancy asked.

"Placed my officers *inside* the house. That way, we can catch the thief as soon as he breaks in. It will be a lot less obvious from the outside, too, since the thief has seen the surveillance car."

Hannah nodded. "I'd feel safer with the police indoors, as long as there isn't any shooting."

"The use of guns shouldn't be necessary," Chief McGinnis told Hannah. He turned to Officers Walker and Daniel. "You'll relieve Rudinsky and Brody. We'll take all of the cars back to the station."

"Do you think the thief will come back tonight?" asked Carson Drew.

"I doubt it," said the chief, "but I don't want to take any chances. Rudinsky, Brody, go home and get some rest. You'll report back here tomorrow afternoon.

"Yes, sir," Sergeant Rudinsky said.

"Pleasant dreams, everyone," Chief McGinnis said.

Nancy, her father, and Hannah headed back into the house, accompanied by Officers Walker and Daniel.

"So we meet again," Rob Walker said to Nancy. "You've had quite a day."

"I'll say," said Jean Daniel. "That was a lucky break you got this afternoon."

Nancy tried to signal to the officers not to discuss the bridge incident, but it was too late.

"What lucky break?" Carson Drew asked, giving Nancy a curious look.

Nancy sighed. There was no point in keeping the story from him any longer. "We had a close call this afternoon on the River Heights Bridge," she said simply.

Hannah gasped. "Is that what Bess meant about your luck running out?"

Nancy nodded, then told them the whole story. She tried to play down the dangerous parts, but there was no fooling either one of them.

"I knew it," Hannah said. "I knew you were hiding something."

Carson Drew gave his daughter a stern look. "You should have told us this before."

"I didn't want you to worry unnecessarily," Nancy told him. "And it was already over. Telling you wouldn't have changed anything."

"I guess not," said Carson, "but we worry anyway." He wrapped his arms tightly around his daughter. "You could have been killed today."

"I'm sorry, Dad. I promise I'll keep you up to date about everything else that happens."

Officers Walker and Daniel made a quick search of the house. "We'll keep watch downstairs," Officer Walker said. "You folks get yourselves a good night's sleep."

"There's no chance in the world I'll sleep tonight," Hannah said. "If this thief is capable of running Nancy off the road, who knows what else he'd do to get the brooch."

"We'll make sure you never have to find out," Officer Daniel said. "You're perfectly safe as long as we're here."

"Thank you again," Nancy said to the officers. "Good night, everybody."

The last thing Nancy heard as she headed up the stairs was Hannah offering to make the police a pot of coffee. Good old Hannah, Nancy thought with a smile.

Nancy changed into her nightgown and climbed

into bed. With the officers downstairs and the thief scared off, at least for the night, she could finally get some sleep. She rested her head on the pillow and closed her eyes, but she couldn't stop thinking about the case.

Lydia, Kimberly Burton, and Russell Brown had all been at the expo and in a position to steal the brooch. Lydia and Mr. Brown had the clearest motivation. Lydia needed start-up money for her business. Mr. Brown had recently taken out an insurance policy and could collect money on the stolen brooch. Lydia had had the best opportunity to hide the brooch inside the clock. She'd been alone at Mr. Gordon's booth right after the robbery was discovered. And while there was still nothing specific tying Kimberly Burton to the case, she had been in the best position to sabotage Nancy's car.

And then there was Henry Gordon. He'd been alone with the clock briefly, but that was before the robbery occurred. True, he'd been insistent about delivering the clock after the expo, but that was entirely consistent with what Nancy knew about him. He was a good businessman. Besides, the police officers tailing him hadn't turned up anything unusual. Nancy wasn't ready to cross his name off the list yet, but he was definitely taking a back seat to the other suspects.

Nancy kept juggling the possibilities, but no clear theory emerged. Something didn't add up. She turned over onto her side and bunched up her pillow.

She really had to go to sleep or she'd be too tired to think. Nancy tried to make her mind go blank, but a question kept appearing: Where had she seen that orange van before?

Nancy rolled over onto her stomach and sighed. At this rate, she'd be up all night.

Nancy awakened to sunlight streaming through her window and turned to look at the clock. It was ten-thirty! She jumped out of bed. She'd overslept, and there was so much to do.

Grabbing her phone, Nancy punched George's number and asked her to pick her up in half an hour. She was sitting on the curb in front of her house, munching a piece of toast, when George and Bess arrived.

"What happened to the police?" Bess asked, nodding toward the vacant spot across the street where the blue sedan had been parked.

Nancy climbed into the back seat. "Hannah's serving them breakfast."

"Does that mean they didn't get the thief?" George asked. "Did someone break in last night?"

"It's a long story," Nancy said. "I'll tell you on the way to Lydia's house."

By the time Nancy had finished telling the cousins the details of the break-in, George was turning onto Lydia's street.

"So you think the thief will come back?" asked George.

"I think so," Nancy replied, "especially now that it looks as if the police are gone."

"Unless the thief decided not to take any more chances," said Bess. "Maybe he's skipped town."

Suddenly George slammed her foot on the brakes. "Doesn't look like it," she said as Nancy and Bess were jerked forward in their seats.

Nancy looked up and saw what had made George react so abruptly. Parked right in front of Lydia's house was an orange van with green stripes.

10

A Moving Story

Nancy stared at the van in amazement. There was no mistaking it. The van looked exactly like the one that had nearly run them off the bridge the day before.

George immediately pulled over to the curb, and the three girls jumped out of the car. As they neared the van, Nancy finally got an answer to one of the questions that had been troubling her. Beneath the three lime green stripes painted along the van's side was a company logo: RapidSend.

"That's it!" Nancy cried. "I can't believe I didn't remember the name. Those vans are all over the city."

"Isn't RapidSend a moving company or something like that?" asked George.

"It is," Bess informed them. "I've seen their ads in the newspaper. Too bad the paper's not in color or I might have recognized the logo. It's hard to forget orange with green stripes."

"But what's a moving truck doing here?" Nancy wondered. "Didn't Lydia say she was living with her parents and that she'd be here for a while? And she just rented a store, so she wouldn't be leaving town."

Looking at Nancy, Bess said, "You know, I didn't want to believe Lydia was capable of breaking the law, but I'm beginning to think you might be right."

"I still might be wrong," Nancy told her. "After all, there's nothing definite pinning her to the crime."

"This van looks pretty definite to me," Bess said, peering through its open side door. "Hey, look at this."

Nancy and George joined Bess. Inside the van they saw several pieces of furniture covered with old blankets.

"Looks as if Lydia's moving out," Bess said.

The sound of voices made the girls turn around. Coming around the side of the Newkirk house were two young men in jeans and orange T-shirts. They were carrying a salmon pink coffee table shaped like an amoeba. Lydia followed right behind. Bright as the orange T-shirts were, they paled next to Lydia's minidress, which was a frantic swirl of hot pink, yellow, turquoise, and lime green. On her feet she wore white boots that reached almost to her knees.

Lydia stopped short when she saw her friends. "Uh-oh . . ."

"Is something wrong?" Bess asked.

Lydia looked nervously at Bess. "No one was supposed to know about this except my parents," she said.

"Your *parents?*" exclaimed Bess. "You mean they're in on it, too?"

"They understand," said Lydia. "Sometimes you have to be a little sneaky to get what you want."

"*A little sneaky?*" Bess echoed again. "That's what you call robbery and attempted murder?"

Lydia looked confused. "What are you talking about?"

"I'm talking about the orange van," Bess said in an accusing tone. "Is that the same one that ran us off the River Heights Bridge yesterday?"

Lydia looked shocked. "I don't understand."

"And *I* don't understand how you can even look me in the face after you tried to kill us," Bess replied.

Noticing that the men in the orange T-shirts had stopped to listen with interest, Lydia directed them to continue moving things into the van. Then she turned to Bess and said, "I don't know what you're talking about."

"You're doing a great job of playing innocent, Lydia," Bess went on angrily. "Do you want me to refresh your memory?" She recounted for Lydia how the orange van had pursued them.

A look of horror came over Lydia's face. "I swear, Bess, it's just a coincidence that I rented this van," she insisted. "I would never do anything so awful."

Bess still looked skeptical. "And I suppose you have a really good alibi ready for us?"

"It's not an alibi. It's the truth. I didn't want to tell you, but if it will clear my name . . ." Lydia looked around as if she was afraid of being overheard. "I'm opening my own antique store on Center Street. It's going to be called the Time Machine."

Nancy, Bess, and George remained silent, waiting to hear what else Lydia would reveal.

"It'll be different from Henry's store," Lydia continued. "It's not going to sell stuff from just one period. I'm going to have displays from different times so you can walk from one to another and feel as if you're traveling through time."

"Is that what that 1950s coffee table is for?" Nancy asked as the two men loaded the irregularly shaped piece into the van.

Lydia nodded. "I rented the van to transport it and my other furniture. I've been collecting stuff now for the past few months. That's what I was really doing at the antiques expo, not shopping for clothes, as I'd said."

"Starting up a business must be pretty expensive," Nancy said. "And you just got out of school. How can you afford it?"

"My parents have given me a loan," Lydia replied. "I'm going to pay it back as soon as I can."

Nancy studied Lydia closely. She seemed to be telling the truth, but now she had a definite reason to have tried to steal the brooch—she had a loan to pay back.

"So why all the secrecy?" George asked. "Starting a business isn't a crime."

Lydia gave them a sheepish look. "I didn't want Henry to know. I was afraid he'd fire me before I was ready to open. I needed the money he paid me, and the experience." She looked at her watch. "Look, I'd like to help you guys, but I've got to return this van in a few hours."

Nancy still wasn't convinced of Lydia's innocence, but she didn't think Lydia was going to reveal anything more, at least not now. There was always the chance that Lydia might drop her guard later on, though, if she thought they believed her. Nancy gave Lydia a big smile. "I'm sorry we came barging over here," she said. "You can understand why we were upset about the van."

"Sure," Lydia said. "I'm really sorry about what you went through, too."

"We'll let you get back to your moving," Nancy said, as she and her friends started to walk toward George's car. "And good luck with your store."

"I can't believe you let her off the hook so easily," Bess said when they'd pulled away. "Did you really believe her story?"

"Yes," said Nancy. "About the store, at least. Everything she said fits with things we already know. The real estate office rented her the store, and she's got all that antique furniture, so she'd need to rent a van."

George looked expectantly at Nancy. "So that's it? We cross her off our list?"

"Well, no," Nancy said. "There are still too many coincidences, like the fact that she's using RapidSend to move her furniture. There are lots of other movers in town. And Lydia had the best opportunity to hide the brooch inside the clock."

"Which means that avoiding Henry Gordon might not be the only reason she's sneaking around," added Bess.

"That's right," Nancy agreed. "If she sold the brooch, she'd be able to pay back her parents and have money left to invest in her business."

"So what's our plan?" asked George.

"We'll go to RapidSend," Nancy told her. "Now that we know what kind of van it was, we should find out who drove or rented one yesterday. Can I borrow your phone?"

George pulled her mobile phone out of its pouch, and Nancy dialed information for RapidSend's address.

"It's just off Route Nine," Nancy said after she hung up.

It was hard to miss the large RapidSend sign, even from a half mile down the road. George turned into a parking lot filled with dozens of identical orange vans and trucks of different sizes.

"It could have been Lydia," George said, eyeing the vans. "Or it could have been about a billion other people."

Nancy bit her lip in frustration. "I don't feel that we're narrowing down our list of suspects."

The girls entered a small square concrete building in the middle of the lot. Inside, a young woman sat behind a desk. She had long, curly hair and wore hoop earrings. Her nameplate read Jolie Wilson.

"Are you here to rent a truck?" she asked.

"No," Nancy said. "We need to talk to the owner or manager of the company right away."

"I'm sorry," said Ms. Wilson. "My father is busy right now and can't be disturbed."

"It's very important," Nancy insisted.

The young woman shrugged. "If you really need to see him personally, you'll have to set up an appointment."

"Look," Nancy said, "I don't want to be a pest, but one of your vans nearly killed us yesterday. If you don't let us see your father, you could be accused of obstructing justice."

Jolie Wilson stood up from the desk and stammered, "I-I'll be right back." She disappeared through a gray metal door and was back in less than a minute. "My father will see you," she said.

Before Nancy, Bess, and George could move, a middle-aged man appeared in the doorway. He was balding and had a mustache. "I'm George Wilson, the owner," the man said, extending his hand. "Please come in."

The girls were led into a large, comfortable office with a glass-topped desk and dark green leather chairs.

"Make yourselves comfortable." Wilson gestured toward the chairs. "Now tell me again what you told my daughter."

Nancy was beginning to lose track of how many times she'd told the story of the orange van, but she repeated it again. Mr. Wilson listened carefully, absently tapping a pencil against his desk.

"There's no way it could have been one of our drivers," Mr. Wilson said when she was finished. "We check them out very carefully. They all have good driving records, and none of them has ever committed a crime."

"Does anyone else drive your vans?" Nancy asked.

"Sometimes our customers do," he replied. "We give them that option."

"We're not accusing anyone of anything," Nancy said. "We'd just like a list of your drivers to see if any of their names correspond to the information we already have."

Mr. Wilson looked Nancy squarely in the eye. "I knew it," he blurted out. "You work for U-Truck-It, don't you?"

"What?" Nancy asked, perplexed.

"U-Truck-It is another moving company. They've been trying to destroy my business for years. Now they're trying to steal my drivers. I won't stand for it. I'll tell you that right now."

"I already told you who we are," Nancy insisted. "We're not trying to steal anyone. We're trying to *catch* a thief!"

"I'm not buying it," Wilson said, tapping his pencil even louder.

"I have a suggestion," Nancy said. "Why don't you call the River Heights chief of police and check out our story? If you're convinced then that we're telling the truth, would you give us a list of your drivers?"

The pencil came to rest at the edge of the desk. "Leave your phone number with Jolie," Mr. Wilson said. "If I'm satisfied with the chief's story, we'll be in touch."

"That Mr. Wilson is one tough customer," Bess said as George parked in front of Nancy's house half an hour later. "I can see why he's so successful. He really stands up for himself."

Nancy was frowning as she got out of the car. "Unless he's protecting one of his drivers."

"Do you think Mr. Wilson might know something he's not telling us?" asked George.

"Maybe," Nancy said. "Or else he's just being cautious."

Bess looked worried. "What if he doesn't call Chief McGinnis? Then we may never find out who was behind the wheel of that van."

"I'll ask Chief McGinnis to call him," Nancy said, unlocking the front door and letting her friends in.

"It was nice of you to invite us for lunch," said Bess. "I feel very deserving today, since I didn't have any ice cream."

Nancy almost laughed out loud when they reached the kitchen. Sergeant Rudinsky, wearing a flowered blouse and jeans, sat across from Officer Brody, who was also in blue jeans. Hannah stood over them with a huge bowl of chicken salad.

"We really shouldn't be eating like this on the job," the sergeant said. "You're distracting us, Ms. Gruen."

"But you'd offend me by refusing," the housekeeper said.

"Well, maybe just a smidge," Sergeant Rudinsky agreed. Hannah spooned chicken salad onto her already overloaded plate.

"Delicious," Officer Brody said through a mouthful of food. "This is a lot better than sitting in that car all day."

"Hi, Hannah. That looks yummy," Nancy said, stepping into the kitchen.

Hannah smiled when she saw the girls. "There's plenty more."

After greeting the officers, Nancy, Bess, and George grabbed some plates and silverware and joined them at the table. They hadn't eaten more than a few mouthfuls when the doorbell rang.

"I'll get it," Nancy said, hopping out of her chair.

She sprinted down the hall and opened the front door, but there was no one there. Nancy stepped outside and looked around. She didn't see anyone in the yard or on the street, either.

That's funny, she thought, turning around to go back inside. Stopping suddenly, Nancy saw a knife sticking into the front of the house, its short, sharp blade pinning a piece of paper next to the door.

Nancy's heartbeat quickened as she ripped the note away from the knife and read it:

> You can't catch me. No one can.
> Tick, tock, I'll get that clock
> With or without you, Nancy Drew!

11

Playing Cat and Mouse

Nancy raced across the lawn to the street. She looked in both directions for an orange van, tire tracks, or any sign of the person who'd left the note. She was sure he couldn't have gone far. Running back to the house, Nancy checked the bushes on either side of the entrance. There was no sign of the thief. He or she seemed to have vanished into thin air.

Nancy read the note again. It was hard to tell whether it meant the thief was going to break in that evening or do something even more desperate to get the clock. Either way, Nancy had a feeling she'd soon come face-to-face with the criminal.

Nancy returned to the front door, yanked the knife out of the wooden shingle, and examined it closely. It was exquisitely crafted, with a mother-of-pearl handle. The blade was no longer shiny, even rusty in places, but it still looked very sharp. Nancy had never seen anything quite like it before.

She turned the knife over in her hand, thinking of Kimberly Burton's collection of swords and daggers. Could this be one of them? And the note said Nancy would never catch the thief. Could this be Kimberly's way of teasing her, since the woman might have gotten away with her crimes before?

Nancy reentered the house and found her purse on the front hall table. Knowing how upset Hannah would be when she saw the note, Nancy hid the knife inside her purse. No need to worry her further, Nancy thought.

"Nancy?" Hannah called.

Nancy jumped, hoping the housekeeper hadn't seen what she'd just done. "Yes?" she asked, turning.

Hannah stood in the doorway to the kitchen, an anxious look on her face. "Who was at the door?" she asked.

"We got another note," she said, walking toward the kitchen. "I'd better show it to the officers."

Officer Rudinsky was on her feet before Nancy even entered the kitchen. She strode toward Nancy, holding her hand out for the note. After she'd read it, she let out a low whistle. "This is very serious."

Officer Brody had also risen from the table and stood behind his partner, reading over her shoulder. Hannah was in the doorway, her arms crossed in front of her chest and her lips pressed together in a thin line. Bess and George looked confused until Sergeant Rudinsky passed the note to them.

"It could actually be a good thing," Nancy said.

Everyone looked at her as if she were crazy.

"Think about it," Nancy said. "The thief would never have come near the house if he thought the police were still here. That means there's a good chance he'll come back tonight."

"And with us inside the house," Officer Brody added, "there's no way he'll get away this time."

"As long as we're not too busy eating on the job," Sergeant Rudinsky said, chuckling.

"Don't torture yourself," Bess said, with a laugh. "You were tempted by Hannah's cooking. I don't think *anyone* could have resisted it." As if to prove her point, she ate another forkful of chicken salad.

"You know, Nancy," George said, "I bet there's something else you can do to help lure the thief here tonight. I thought of it while I was reading the note. It sounds like the thief is trying to scare you. So what if you act scared?"

Bess paused, her fork in midair. "Huh?"

"Make it look as if you're too scared to stay in the house tonight," George explained.

"That's a great idea," Nancy agreed excitedly. "We could make a big show of leaving—Hannah, my dad, and I. We could turn out the lights, drive the car a couple of blocks away, then sneak back in."

"Oh, I get it," said Bess. "The thief will think the Drews *and* the police are gone."

Sergeant Rudinsky nodded. "It makes sense," she said. "We can let you in through the back door. Unless you'd rather stay away all night, of course."

"I never thought I'd say this," Hannah said slowly, "but I'd rather come home. Even if the thief does show up, I'd feel safer here in the house with the police than I would anywhere else."

"Then it's settled," Nancy said.

"What's next, Nancy?" asked George. "Do we just wait for tonight?"

Nancy shook her head. "No. I think it's time we paid another visit to Kimberly Burton."

"It sure looks old," said Bess. She was in the back seat of George's car, examining the pearl-handled knife. "Do you think it might be one of Kimberly's?"

"That's what I want to find out," Nancy said.

"She does have a big collection of weapons," Bess recalled with a shiver.

Nancy had called ahead, saying she wanted to take another look at Kimberly's globe brooch. When the girls pulled up in front of the big stone house, Kimberly was waiting for them with the front door open.

"I knew we'd meet again," she said.

Nancy felt uneasy as she introduced George. Again she found herself searching Kimberly's face for some double meaning. Why was Kimberly so sure they'd be back? Was she simply confident about her jewelry, or had she set it up so the girls would *have* to come back?

Determined not to show her uncertainty, Nancy decided to play along with Kimberly. "Isn't it funny how certain paths seem to cross?" Nancy commented.

"Life is full of surprises," said Kimberly, looking right into Nancy's eyes. "Don't you think?"

"Oh, I try never to be surprised," Nancy said lightly. "I like to stay one step ahead."

"Not this time," Kimberly said. She motioned for the girls to follow her down the hall. "I'm the only one who knows where my office is, so you'll have to follow me."

Nancy sneaked a glance at George and Bess, who both looked as puzzled with the woman's behavior as Nancy was.

Kimberly led the girls down the same hallway they'd passed through before, the one decorated with tapestries and suits of armor. Up ahead, Nancy saw the wall covered with ancient weapons. Though Kimberly started to walk past it, Nancy stopped.

"This is quite a collection," Nancy said, quickly scanning the wall to see if one of the knives was missing. There were no empty spaces, but several of the knives had pearl handles. "Do you have any more like this?" she asked, pointing to the knife most similar to the one in her purse.

Kimberly frowned. "I thought you came here to discuss brooches, not knives," she said.

108

"I'm like you," Nancy said coolly. "I have many interests."

"My knives are not for sale," Kimberly said firmly. Then her golden cat's eyes crinkled at the corners and almost gleamed. "But sometimes I choose to give one away," she said, "to one of my special friends."

What did she mean by "special friends"? Nancy wondered. Did she mean she'd "given" the knife to Nancy by sticking it in the Drews' house?

Kimberly turned her back on the girls and led them to a different room from the one they'd been in the day before. This one, despite its stone walls, was a modern office furnished with the latest technology, including a computer, a laser printer, and a fax machine. As in the sitting room, there was a table covered with a red velvet cloth.

This time Kimberly didn't leave the room to get her jewelry collection. She unlocked a heavy wooden cabinet and removed the same wooden tray Nancy and Bess had seen before. On it, among the necklaces and bracelets, was the globe brooch with its amber and emerald continents and sapphire oceans.

As Nancy picked up the brooch to study it, she came up with one last ploy. "You know," she said, "this brooch is beautiful, but I've recently seen a similar piece that's a little nicer."

"Similar?" Kimberly asked with interest. "What does it look like?"

Nancy described the rose brooch's ruby petals and emerald stem.

"I'd love to get my hands on that," Kimberly said, her eyes gleaming. "Do you know where I might find it? I know you saw it first, but you don't mind a little competition, do you?"

It was exactly the reaction Nancy had been hoping for, and yet she was still dissatisfied. Kimberly could have said she wanted to find the brooch to hide the fact that she herself had stolen it. Or she might have been simply interested in acquiring another piece of jewelry.

For good measure, Nancy decided to make her position clear. "I'm afraid I do mind," she said. "The brooch may never be mine, but it certainly won't be yours."

"Don't bet on it," Kimberly said with a wink. "I can be very persuasive." Standing up, she said briskly, "Well, if we can't do business, may I bid you a fond farewell?"

Kimberly led the girls back into the hallway. As they approached the front door, she gave them one last grin. "Who knows when our paths will cross again?"

"My head is reeling," Nancy said to Bess and George as they drove home. "Everything Kimberly said made her sound guilty. But I'm still not sure she's done anything wrong."

"She's a puzzle, all right," George agreed. "I sure hope your thief comes through tonight, or we may never get any answers to this case."

110

"Yeah," said Bess. "We've never worked on a case where there were so many people who seemed guilty."

George dropped Nancy in front of her house. "Call me tonight if anything happens," she said. "I don't care how late it is."

"Me, too," Bess said. "I'm sure I won't be sleeping, anyway. I'll be too busy wondering what's going on."

Carson Drew arrived home an hour after Nancy. They waited with Hannah until it began to get dark, then put George's plan into action. After turning out all the lights, Nancy and her father left the house in his car, followed by Hannah in her station wagon. They parked on a side street several blocks away, then came back on foot, cutting through a neighbor's backyard and staying in the shadows. They reentered the house through the back door.

Officer Brody, waiting at the kitchen table, stood up abruptly when they entered, and his hand went to his revolver. When he saw them, he relaxed. "I'm glad you're back," he said. "Now we can lock up and wait."

Hannah went to the refrigerator and pulled out some sandwiches. "We can eat while we're waiting."

Nancy helped Hannah bring the sandwiches and pitchers of juice to the darkened living room, where Sergeant Rudinsky sat, ready for action.

Rudinsky roamed the first floor while Nancy, her father, Hannah, and Officer Brody ate in the semi-darkness. They were careful to keep the curtains drawn and to speak in whispers so that they couldn't be detected from outside the house.

Soon it was almost pitch black in the living room. The darkness and quiet were so peaceful that Nancy was finding it harder and harder to keep her eyes open.

The house was so still that a slight rustling in the bushes had the effect of a firecracker going off. All around her, Nancy could hear the shifting of bodies and rapid breathing. Was this the moment they'd all been waiting for, or was it just a squirrel or a raccoon?

The squeaking of a living room window being opened answered Nancy's question. Nancy held her breath as the curtains parted, revealing a dark figure silhouetted against a triangle of night sky. First one leg came over the windowsill, then another.

Nancy's heart pounded as she saw that the thief was inside the house. The figure hesitated by the window before taking a few steps toward them.

Then everything happened at once. The window was slammed shut and the lights were turned on. Officer Brody drew his gun and yelled, "Freeze!"

It took a moment for Nancy's eyes to adjust to the sudden bright light. But when they did, she could only stare at the frightened figure standing in her living room. It was Russell Brown!

12

An Answer Too Late

Russell Brown squinted at the bright light through his horn-rimmed glasses. When he caught Nancy's eye, he looked away.

"We caught him!" cried Officer Brody, whipping out a pair of handcuffs. As he snapped the cuffs on the unresisting Brown, Sergeant Rudinsky approached, gun drawn.

"You can put that down, Officer," Brown said, so quietly that Nancy barely heard him. "I won't put up a fight."

Nodding curtly, Sergeant Rudinsky replaced the gun in her holster. "You have the right to remain silent," she began to recite. "Anything you say can and will be used against you in a court of law."

"I'm not going to remain silent," Brown said, a little

more force in his voice now. "I'm innocent, no matter what you might think."

Rudinsky droned on, ignoring him. "You have the right to an attorney. If you cannot afford an attorney, one—"

"Just listen to me," Brown insisted. "You don't understand what happened."

After reading Brown his rights the police officer fell silent.

Brown asked, "Now can I talk?"

"As long as you understand what I've just said," answered Sergeant Rudinsky.

"Yes, yes, I've seen all the cop shows," Brown said. "But let me explain. I admit I broke in tonight—"

"Hard to deny," Nancy observed.

Brown looked at Nancy as he went on. "I was just trying to get the brooch back before the *real* thief stole it. It is mine, after all."

"But why did you have to break in?" Nancy asked. "Why didn't you go to the police and ask for the brooch back?"

"It's very complicated," Brown mumbled.

"Does it have anything to do with an insurance policy?" asked Nancy.

Brown looked shocked, then tried to cover his reaction. "I don't know what you're talking about," he sputtered.

"I think you do," Nancy said smoothly. "I saw the fifty-thousand-dollar insurance policy you took out on the brooch right before it was stolen."

"You had no business nosing around my store," he said, his face reddening.

"It was in plain view," said Nancy. "You should have made more effort to hide it. I think I know the real reason you're here tonight. You wanted to make it look as if the brooch really *was* stolen so you could collect the insurance money. Then, maybe a few years down the line, when everyone had forgotten about it, you could sell the brooch and get another fifty thousand."

For a moment Brown just glared at Nancy. Then his stare wavered and his shoulders slumped. "I *need* the money. My business is going under. I haven't sold anything in months."

"That was you who broke in last night, too?" Nancy asked Brown.

"Yes," he admitted. "I should have given up while I was ahead."

"What about the orange van?" asked Nancy.

Brown's face showed no reaction. "What orange van?" he asked.

"The one that tried to run us off the bridge," Nancy explained patiently. "A couple of hours before we came to your store."

"I have no idea what you're talking about," Brown said indignantly. "I'm at my store every day from ten o'clock until six. I certainly can't afford to hire any help."

"What about this knife?" Nancy asked, pulling it from her purse.

Behind Nancy, Hannah gasped. "Where did you get that?" the housekeeper asked.

"The second note was stuck to our house with this knife," Nancy explained.

"I don't know anything about a knife or a note," Brown insisted. "I'm just a common burglar, I guess." He laughed without humor.

Nancy watched Brown's expression carefully. She knew he wasn't a trustworthy person, but she had the feeling he was telling the truth about the knife and the van. Now she was beginning to believe there was more than one person after the brooch. And it looked as if the second person was playing a lot dirtier than Brown was.

"Is there anything else you want to ask the suspect?" Officer Brody asked Nancy.

Nancy shook her head.

"Let's book him," Sergeant Rudinsky said, taking Brown by the arm. She radioed the station on her walkie-talkie. "Rudinsky here. Request vehicle to pick us up at the Drew home. We have caught the intruder."

"Roger, Rudinsky," came the answer over the walkie-talkie. "Chief McGinnis asked us to tell you he'll be coming over himself."

"Roger," the sergeant said.

A few minutes later the doorbell rang. Brody opened it to the chief of police.

"Brown!" Chief McGinnis exclaimed as he entered the living room. "So it was you."

Brown cast his eyes downward as Nancy filled the chief in on the night's incidents.

As the officers led Russell Brown away, Hannah sighed with relief. "Now I can finally feel safe in my own home," she said.

Carson Drew smiled and put an arm around Nancy. "Good work," he said. "You've caught the criminal, and we're all still in one piece."

Nancy smiled uneasily. She didn't want her father and Hannah to worry any more than they already had, but she didn't want them to have a false sense of security, either. Briefly, she told them of her suspicion that someone besides Brown was after the brooch.

"Well," Carson said when she had explained, "I guess the first thing we'd better do is get the police back in here."

Nancy hurried outside to Chief McGinnis, who was getting into his car. She quickly explained her suspicions.

The police chief nodded. "Rudinsky, you stay here until we send backup," he instructed the sergeant.

Nancy was relieved that at least her father and Hannah would feel safer now. But Nancy knew she wouldn't rest easily until she had managed to figure out exactly who the second suspect was.

Early the next morning, George and Bess picked up Nancy at her house. The three girls drove to the

Frosty Freeze plant so George could begin her day's work.

"Thanks again for the car," Nancy said as George got out. "Mine should be out of the shop tomorrow."

"No problem," George said. "Just pick me up here at five."

As Nancy and Bess drove home, Bess yawned. "That was quite a night you had. Even I'm tired from all the excitement."

"I'm sorry I called you so late," Nancy told her friend, "but you said you wanted to know what happened."

"Oh, I did," Bess assured her. "Don't apologize. I'm just glad they caught the crook."

"I'm not so sure the case is closed," Nancy said. She repeated for Bess her fear that there was a second thief.

"I don't know," Bess said, shaking her head. "Russell Brown could be lying about the knife and the notes. Maybe he doesn't want to get in any more trouble than he's already in."

Nancy shook her head. "I have a feeling about this," she said. "I don't think he was lying."

When Nancy and Bess arrived at the Drews' house, they found Officers Walker and Daniel pacing the living room.

"What's going on?" Nancy asked them.

"Not much," Officer Walker replied. "Your housekeeper had to go out, but she left you a note on the kitchen table."

118

"More notes," Nancy said with a groan. "I hope this one's good news." With Bess in tow, Nancy headed for the kitchen and found a sheet of paper on the table. "All right!" she exclaimed.

"What is it?" asked Bess.

Nancy waved the paper in the air. "George Wilson called us back. I guess he believed us after all." Grabbing the receiver of the wall phone, she punched out the number Hannah had written on the note. "Hi, Jolie, it's Nancy Drew," Nancy said into the receiver. "I'm returning your father's call."

Jolie replied, "I have the information you requested, those names of drivers who had our trucks out the day before yesterday," she told Nancy. "Would you like me to mail you the list?"

"That would take too long," said Nancy. "Could you read the names over the phone?" She pulled a notebook and pencil out of her purse.

"Sure. They're in alphabetical order. Dennis Abrams, Jackie Bitterman, Lisa Cortes . . ."

Nancy jotted down the names as fast as she could while Jolie continued.

"Marco Roggero, Alastair Short, Lee Thompson . . ."

Thompson! Nancy stopped writing. Thompson was the last name of the woman who'd owned the rose brooch. Was this just a coincidence? Nancy was itching to get off the phone, but she forced herself to write down the rest of the names in case any of the others were significant.

119

"Thanks very much," said Nancy after Jolie had finished. "And please tell your father that we won't share this information with anyone but the police."

"Thanks. And I'm really sorry it was one of our vans that came after you," Jolie said. "Please call us if it *was* one of our drivers. I'm sure my father would want to know."

"Sure," Nancy agreed.

After she'd hung up, she raced upstairs to her bedroom with Bess close behind.

"So what did you find out?" Bess demanded, breathless from hurrying after Nancy.

Nancy started rummaging through a pile of papers on her desk. "I need the list from the expo," she mumbled. "One of the drivers who works for Mr. Wilson is named Lee Thompson."

Bess gave her a blank look.

"The brooch originally belonged to Agnes Thompson," Nancy explained. "This could be the lead we've been waiting for."

She located the two lists she'd borrowed from Mary Lou Jennings and handed one to Bess.

"Thompson, Thompson," Bess murmured, running her finger down the page of names. Nancy did the same with the other list.

"I've got it!" Nancy exclaimed. "Here it is on the second page."

Bess looked over Nancy's shoulder. "It *has* to be more than a coincidence," she said. "Thompson's not

120

a very unusual name, but I'll bet there's a connection."

"I know the man who's going to help us make that connection," Nancy said, snapping her fingers. "And right now he's behind bars at the River Heights police station."

"Russell Brown," said Bess, reading Nancy's thoughts. "Let's go!"

The girls were almost out the door when the phone rang.

"Oh, rats, I forgot to turn the answering machine on," Nancy said. "I'll be right back." She ran into the kitchen.

Grabbing the receiver, Nancy said, "Hello?"

At first no one said anything, but Nancy could hear breathing on the other end of the line.

"Hello?" she repeated. "Is someone there?"

"Is this Nancy Drew?" asked a gruff, unfamiliar male voice.

Nancy didn't like the sound of the voice, but she remained calm. "Yes," she responded.

"This is what you're going to do," the man said. "You and your blond friend are going to bring the brooch to the intersection of Route Nine and Route Twenty-two in fifteen minutes."

Nancy drew in a sharp breath. She'd been right about another thief being after the brooch. And she'd have bet anything that the man on the other end of the telephone line was Lee Thompson!

Stalling to give herself time to think, Nancy said, "And what if we don't?"

"That's easy," the man said. "If you don't bring me the brooch, you'll never see your friend George alive again."

13

Time Runs Out

Nancy clutched the receiver so hard her fingers turned white. If only I had made the connection about Lee Thompson earlier, Nancy thought, before he got hold of George. If she let Thompson know she was on to him now, he might injure George, or worse.

"Who is it?" asked Bess, coming back into the kitchen.

Nancy shook her head and put a finger to her lips.

"Is something wrong?" Bess asked, more anxiously.

At the same time, the gruff male voice spoke up over the phone. "Are you there?"

Shooting Bess a helpless look, Nancy said into the mouthpiece, "Yes, I'm here."

"The clock is ticking," the man said. He gave a sinister laugh that made Nancy shiver. Then he added, "Only fourteen minutes left. And don't even *think* about bringing the police with you. If anyone follows you, you won't see your friend George ever again."

"I understand," Nancy said. Her mind was racing, trying to figure out a way around the caller's demand. Maybe she could phone Chief McGinnis and tell him where they were meeting the kidnapper. That way, the police could show up right after she'd handed over the brooch—or at least follow the man when he tried to escape.

As if he'd read her mind, the caller said, "It won't matter if the police know where you're meeting me. That's not our final destination."

Nancy shuddered at the words "final destination." "We'll be there," she said tersely, then hung up.

"What? What?" asked Bess, hanging on Nancy's arm.

"Thompson's got George," Nancy said quietly. "At least, I'm pretty sure it's Thompson."

"Got? What does that mean, 'got'?"

"It means he wants the brooch in"—Nancy checked her watch—"thirteen minutes or he's going to hurt George." Nancy didn't want to say "kill" for fear of worrying Bess more than she already was.

"Oh, no!" Bess cried, pacing back and forth between the kitchen counter and the table. "Can't we take Officers Walker and Daniel with us? They're right here."

"No," Nancy said as she punched out Chief

McGinnis's direct line. "Thompson warned me not to."

The chief of police picked up the phone and said, "McGinnis here."

As quickly as she could, Nancy explained the situation and what she'd learned about Thompson.

"What if we hid an officer in the back seat of your car?" McGinnis suggested.

"I'm too afraid of what might happen to George if the timing's not exactly right," said Nancy. "What about the police helicopter? That way you could see where we go after we meet Thompson at the intersection."

"Too loud and noticeable," the chief said. "Thompson would be sure to see it. I wish there were time to get you a transmitter. That way we could track you electronically."

Nancy glanced at her watch again. "There's no time for anything," she said urgently. "We've got twelve minutes left."

"Okay, here's what we'll do," said Chief McGinnis. "I'll station unmarked cars north, south, east, and west of the intersection. That way we can intercept you no matter which way you go. I only wish I knew what kind of vehicle to look for."

"It could be anything," Nancy said. "An orange van or maybe Thompson's car."

"We'll find you," Chief McGinnis reassured her. "Now, get going."

Nancy hung up and threw George's car keys to Bess. "Start the car," she said. "I'll be right there."

Nancy raced to her father's study. Her fingers shook as she turned the combination lock. Seconds later, the safe door glided open, and Nancy grabbed the brooch. Then she slammed the door shut and ran into the front hall.

"What's wrong?" Officer Daniel asked, coming from the living room.

"No time to explain," Nancy said breathlessly. "Call Chief McGinnis! He'll tell you everything." Then, as fast as she could, Nancy ran outside to the car.

Bess slid over to let her friend climb in behind the wheel. In a flash, Nancy jerked the gearshift into drive and rammed her foot on the accelerator.

"At least you know the police won't stop you for speeding," Bess said in a shaky voice as they barreled down Nancy's street. She tried to smile, then began to chew her fingernails. "Oh, I hope George is all right. Do you think he's done anything to her?"

"Not yet," Nancy said grimly as she made a sharp left turn. "He's got to give us George or he won't get the brooch."

Nancy made another left onto Route 9 and dodged around slower cars as she drove by fast-food restaurants, shopping malls, and car dealerships.

Traffic thinned as they began to pass more and more empty lots, then farmland. By the time Route 9 ended at the intersection of Route 22, it was completely deserted. Route 22 was a narrow country road with scraggly trees growing on either side. Nancy slowed the car to a stop.

"Where are they?" Bess asked nervously, craning her neck to look out the window.

Nancy got out of the car. Placing her hand above her eyes to shield them from the bright sun, she looked up and down both Route 22 and Route 9. "No sign of them yet," she said.

Then Nancy heard a familiar tinkling tune. Looking down Route 22, she saw the square, white Frosty Freeze ice cream truck bumping and shaking over the uneven dirt road.

"I can't believe I ever liked that song," Bess muttered to herself. She, too, got out of the car.

As the ice cream truck drew closer, Nancy made out a slim, dark-haired figure at the wheel who had to be George. A big, burly form in an orange shirt was beside her in the passenger seat. Nancy blinked as the realization hit her. She'd seen the man at the antiques expo. He had been at Russell Brown's display, wearing the same orange shirt he had on now. An orange shirt just like the ones she'd seen on the RapidSend movers helping Lydia.

When the truck stopped, Nancy saw that the burly man was holding a gun to George's side.

"Oh, George!" Bess cried, running toward the truck.

"Don't come any closer," warned the man in a gruff voice that Nancy recognized from the phone call.

Though he was seated, Nancy could tell he was very tall. His big potbelly stretched the front of his orange T-shirt and hung over his belt. Three faded green stripes ran across the man's flabby chest with the RapidSend logo beneath them.

Nancy was relieved that Bess had obeyed the man and stopped short. Both girls stood very still while the man pushed George out of the truck, his gun still pointing at her ribs. Nancy could see the scared look in George's brown eyes, even though she was acting calm.

"Let me have the brooch," he said, holding out one hand.

Nancy had no choice. She removed the brooch from her purse and placed it in the man's palm. He shoved it in his pocket. As Nancy was closing her purse, she noticed the pearl-handled knife, but realized there was no way she could use it to protect herself and her friends.

"You two," the man said, gesturing at Nancy and Bess with his gun. "Get in the back of the truck."

Nancy and Bess scrambled behind the front seats and waited.

"You drive," the man instructed George. He got into the back with Nancy and Bess. "If you pull any fast moves, your friends will pay for it."

George nodded and got behind the wheel.

"Now go where I told you," the man said to George.

Nancy tried not to look at the gun that pointed first

at her, then at Bess, as the man kept shifting his aim. "Where are we going?" she asked.

"You'll see soon enough," he said. He gave them an eerie smile, then wiped his brow with his free hand. "Sure is hot out," he said. "Bet you'd love to get out of this heat."

"I'd love to get out of here, that's for sure," Nancy told him. She spoke boldly, figuring the man already had a plan and nothing she could say would make it worse. "Who are you?" she demanded.

"Allow me to introduce myself," he said with mock politeness. "The name's Thompson."

Out of the corner of her eye, Nancy could see Bess shoot her a knowing look. Nancy didn't acknowledge it, though. She still didn't want to give Thompson any indication that they already knew who he was.

"How do you do," said Nancy. "I don't suppose you'd like to tell us why you're so interested in that brooch."

"I'm interested in it because it's mine," the man told her. "Or it would have been if that little weasel hadn't cheated me out of what I already owned."

"Who are you talking about?" Nancy asked.

"That skinny little fella with the big glasses," Thompson said bitterly. "Russell Brown."

Nancy was pretty sure she knew what had happened, but she needed to buy time. Maybe getting Thompson to talk more would make him drop his guard. "Mr. Brown cheated you?" she asked. "How?"

"The brooch belonged to my aunt Agnes," Thompson said bitterly. "She was a widow with no children, so when she died, she left me everything. Not that there was much. But she had lots of jewelry, worthless stuff mostly, or at least that's what I thought." Thompson half rose to see how far the truck had gone. "Almost there," he said with satisfaction.

Nancy didn't bother to ask where they were. She knew she'd find out sooner than she wanted to. She didn't have long to distract him, but she decided to try to get the rest of Thompson's story from him.

"So you took the jewelry to Russell Brown?" she prompted.

"That's what I did," he said, nodding. "He told me the whole lot wasn't worth more than a hundred dollars. I didn't know any better—it was all dusty and old. I figured a hundred dollars was better than nothing. Then my sister and her husband dragged me to that expo thing over at the high school, and what do I see? That worm cheated me out of fifty thousand dollars! My sister said I ought to sue him, but I figure I'll just keep things nice and simple and take back what is rightfully mine."

"But you never got a chance to take the piece out of the expo," Nancy said, "because Russell Brown noticed the brooch was gone and called for the police."

"That's right," Thompson said, frowning. "Good thing your clock was sitting right there with that secret compartment. Are you really a detective?" he asked, his bitter expression fading for a moment.

Nancy shrugged. "At the moment I'm just a hostage."

Thompson's bitterness returned. "You got that right. You stupid teenagers didn't even know I was following you," he sneered. "But you still managed to make things difficult for me, didn't you?" He let out a weary sigh. "When the clock wasn't at your friend Gordon's store, I knew you had it."

Nancy shot Bess a quick glance. So Thompson was the one who broke into Past Perfect.

"You should have taken the hint when I trashed your car engine," Thompson went on, speaking as if he were scolding a young child. "But no, you had to play tough—even after I almost pushed you off that bridge."

He aimed the gun toward Bess. Nancy saw that she was trembling and had tears in her eyes.

As George turned up a hill, Thompson cleared his throat. "Enough chitchat," he said gruffly. "Now stay down," he warned Nancy and Bess. "If you say one word or show your face, it will be the last thing you ever do."

Nancy and Bess crouched down as low as they could behind the front seats. The truck came to a stop. A minute later Nancy could hear George talking to a man. Then the truck started slowly up another hill before leveling off. George made a sharp turn and then put on the brakes and turned off the ignition.

When she stepped outside, Nancy immediately realized that they were in the Frosty Freeze parking

131

lot. George usually parked by the large buildings near the driveway, but this time she had stopped at the other end of the vast lot, near one of the smaller buildings. This end of the lot was empty of cars and people. Nancy's hopes sank as she scanned the deserted area.

"That way," Thompson told the three girls, gesturing with his gun toward a door in one of the nearest buildings. "If any of you try to run, you know what will happen to the others."

Nancy was the first to reach the gray padlocked door, and she saw that the lock had been forced open.

"Make a left," Thompson directed as Nancy opened the door.

She obeyed, walking down a wide, empty hallway. Large white doors were set at regular intervals along either side of the corridor. Nancy looked around desperately for a Frosty Freeze employee, but the building was clearly deserted.

"Isn't this building perfect?" Thompson asked as he walked behind them. "I found it this morning. It's empty, but the equipment still works."

"What is this?" Nancy asked with annoyance. She'd come close to solving this crime, but now she felt absolutely helpless.

"The perfect place to put my witnesses on ice," Thompson said.

A cold chill came over Nancy as she began to guess his meaning. Before she could do or say anything,

Thompson instructed the girls to halt next to one of the white doors.

"In you go," he said, opening the door.

Thompson roughly pushed first Nancy, then Bess and George, inside, banging the heavy door shut behind them.

As frigid air washed over the three girls, Nancy knew her worst fears had been realized. They were locked inside a giant ice cream freezer, and no one knew where they were.

14

Deep Freeze

Before she'd even gotten her bearings, Nancy started to shiver. Slapping her arms to keep warm, she looked around the freezer. It was the size of a small room, roughly ten feet square. The ceiling was so low that Nancy could almost reach it if she stood on tiptoe. Stacked against the far wall were several dozen brown cardboard boxes with the Frosty Freeze logo printed on them, along with the slogan, "It's Fr-fr-fr-fr-frosty good!"

George noticed the slogan at the same time Nancy did. "It's frosty, all right," George said grimly, rubbing her arms. "But it's definitely *not* good."

Bess walked closer to the boxes and examined them. "Rocket Pops, Chocosicles, Strawberry Creme-wiches," she read. "You know, this was always a fantasy of mine. All the ice cream I could eat for free." Her round face twisted in a grimace. "Now it seems more like a nightmare."

"There's got to be a way out," Nancy said firmly. "And I'm going to try the most logical one." She grabbed the metal handle of the freezer door and pushed down on it, but the door stayed firmly shut.

"I'm sure Thompson's locked it from the outside," George said. "He took my cordless phone, too."

"What happened?" Nancy asked. "How did he find you?"

"It was right after you dropped me off this morning," George began. "I'd just gotten into my truck and was driving across the parking lot when I saw this guy lying on the pavement as if he was hurt. No one else was around, so I got out to see if I could help. As soon as I knelt down beside him, he jumped up, grabbed my arm, and pulled out a gun!"

Bess's hands flew to her mouth. "Oh, how horrible!" she exclaimed.

"Then what happened?" Nancy asked.

"He made me get behind the wheel and drive the truck past the security booth while he hid in the back. Then, when we were a couple of miles down the road, we pulled over and he called you on my mobile phone."

Nancy shook her head. "I saw him in that orange shirt at the expo," she told the others. "I only wish I'd made the connection before."

"It's not your fault," George told her. "How could you have known that out of all those people, that one guy would turn out to be such a creep?"

"That's right," agreed Bess. "And at least now the mystery is solved."

"Too bad we're the only ones who know that," Nancy pointed out. "And if Thompson gets his way, no one else will ever find out."

Bess began to jump up and down to stay warm. Nancy saw that her skin was becoming very white.

"I hate to say this," Bess said, "but if we don't find a way out of here, Frosty Freeze is going to have three new flavors: Nancy, Bess, and George."

Nancy made an effort to remain calm. "Okay," she said, "let's explore every inch of this place. Look for an emergency exit, an alarm, a removable panel— anything that might be another way out. Above all, stay warm!"

"That's not going to be easy in this outfit," Bess said, looking down at her red and white sundress. "You know, my mother's always telling me to take a sweater in case there's air conditioning. I wish I'd listened to her."

Nancy saw that Bess's shoulders and arms were covered with goose bumps. "This is the strongest air conditioning I've ever felt," Nancy joked, looking down at the freezing skin on her own bare arms and legs. She was wearing a short-sleeved shirt and shorts.

"At least you've got some sort of sleeve," Bess said to Nancy.

"Here," said George, removing her white Frosty Freeze smock and placing it over Bess's shoulders. "I've got on a long-sleeved shirt and pants."

Glad that Bess was better protected against the cold, Nancy turned her attention back to possible escape routes. "Let's spread out," she said. "I'll take the far wall. You two take the side walls." She dragged the boxes of ice cream away from the wall so she could check behind them. The boxes were heavy, but at least the effort was warming her up a little.

To her dismay, Nancy found nothing on the wall but a thermostat—which read zero degrees Fahrenheit. There was no way they could survive very long at such a temperature, even if they did move around.

"Find anything?" George called through the frosty air.

"Not yet," Nancy answered, pushing a stack of boxes in front of the thermostat. She didn't see any reason to tell her friends how bad the situation really was. "How about you?" she asked George.

"Nothing," replied George glumly. "I would have thought they'd put an alarm in here in case someone got locked in."

"You mean like this?" Bess asked, pointing to a small red box in the center of the wall she was checking.

"That's it!" George exclaimed, running forward.

Nancy joined her friends and examined the box. It had a red metal frame around a pane of glass, behind

137

which was a red button. A small sign next to the box read, In Case of Emergency, Break Glass.

"If this isn't an emergency, I don't know what is," said Nancy.

Bess's nervous gaze darted around the room. "But what can we break it with?" she asked. "We need something heavy."

"I've got an idea," Nancy said, removing the pearl-handled knife from her purse. "Let's try this. It didn't save us before, but maybe it will now."

Grabbing the hilt of the knife, Nancy banged the blunt end of the handle against the glass. Nothing happened.

"Harder, Nancy," Bess urged.

"Stand clear," said Nancy. "I don't want to hit you with the blade."

George and Bess stepped back, and again Nancy smashed the handle against the alarm. This time the glass shattered. Nancy gingerly picked pieces of broken glass out of the frame and pushed the button.

"I don't hear anything," Bess said after a few seconds.

"Maybe it's a silent alarm," George suggested hopefully.

Nancy frowned as she spotted something behind the box's metal frame. "I think it's more like a false alarm," she said. Grimly she pulled a handful of loose wires from the back of the box.

"What's that?" asked Bess.

138

"These are supposed to hook up the alarm to the electrical system," Nancy told her. "It looks as if they were never connected."

"Great," said George. "We're stuck in deep freeze because some electrician was too lazy to do his job."

"Don't say that," Nancy said quickly. "We'll find another way out. Let's try the door. There's a pane of glass in it. Maybe we can break it the way we did this one."

Again grabbing the hilt of the knife, Nancy banged away at the glass as hard as she could, but it stayed intact.

"It's probably shatterproof," George said.

"Maybe I can pry it away from the door," suggested Nancy, turning the knife around. The edge of the window was lined with black rubber. With the sharp end of the knife, Nancy tried to separate the rubber from the glass.

"Any luck?" Bess asked after a few minutes.

Nancy shook her head. "The glass goes too far into the frame for me to get at the edges."

"Then we're stuck here," Bess said anxiously. "We'll never get out." She was rubbing her hands together, and Nancy noticed that both Bess's and George's teeth were starting to chatter. Nancy knew that as soon as she stopped moving around so vigorously, she would be in the same shape as her friends.

Turning to George, Nancy asked hurriedly, "Is this building as abandoned as it looks?"

George nodded. "This is just an annex to the main freezer. Surplus is stored here, so it's hardly ever used."

Bess sat down on one of the cardboard boxes and let her head fall into her hands. "What should we do?" she asked desperately.

"Someone will find us," said Nancy with more confidence than she felt. "The police are only a few miles from here, and now they know Thompson's the one who did it. They'll find him, get him to confess, and come rescue us."

"How will they find Thompson?" George asked. "They won't know which way he went, and they don't know what he's driving. Even if they *do* catch him, he might not tell them where we are."

"I can't feel my fingers anymore," said Bess quietly. She held up her hand. "Look, they're turning blue."

"The police *will* find us," Nancy repeated. "And in the meantime there's still one thing we can do."

"What's that?" asked George.

"Keep moving," Nancy said. "The longer we stay warm, the better our chances. So get up!"

"My feet feel as if they're burning," Bess complained. "It hurts to put weight on them."

"Up!" Nancy prodded. "Start doing jumping jacks. That should bring them back to life."

Reluctantly, Bess and George rose, and the three of them began their calisthenics.

"I'm so glad no one can see us in here," George

gasped as they jumped up and down. "This must look so ridiculous."

"It's not ridiculous if it saves our lives," Nancy said, also breathing with difficulty. The air was so cold that it was painful to inhale it into her lungs.

"I'm getting so tired," Bess gasped after several minutes. "My feet feel better, but I can't breathe."

"We can't keep this up too much longer," George agreed. "Maybe we could huddle together for body warmth."

Though Nancy didn't want to give up, her body gave her no choice. "Okay," she said, "but after we rest awhile, we're going to get up again. We can keep jumping and resting until someone comes for us."

Bess sat down on a box of ice cream. George and Nancy sat on either side of her.

"Let's share George's smock," Bess offered, spreading it out over the three of them.

Nancy clutched the edge of the white smock with one hand and placed her other arm over Bess's shoulders. Bess's skin felt like ice.

"Together till the end, right?" said George, giving Nancy a wry smile.

"It's not the end," Nancy insisted. "You'll see."

Actually, she was beginning to feel the same hopelessness Bess and George were feeling, but she knew she had to fight it as long as she could.

"I-it's ironic, wh-when you think about it," Bess said through chattering teeth.

"What is?" Nancy asked.

"The old clock was your first case. Now it may be your—"

"Don't say it," Nancy cut in. It just *couldn't* be my last, Nancy thought, not yet.

"I'm j-just going to c-close my eyes for a bit," Bess said wearily. "Maybe if I take a n-nap, I'll have more energy later."

"Don't close your eyes," Nancy warned, shaking Bess. She knew the most dangerous thing a person could do in subfreezing temperatures was fall asleep. "You've got to stay awake," Nancy told her. Even as she said this, she fought her own urge to yawn.

"Maybe a nap isn't such a bad idea," George said. "If we're sleeping, the time will pass quicker."

"Try!" Nancy pleaded. "Keep your eyes open."

"I'll just sleep for a minute, Nance," Bess said groggily, her eyelids drooping.

This time the desire to yawn was too powerful to resist. Nancy took in a deep breath of frosty air. Maybe she should listen to her body and take a little nap, she thought. The box was more comfortable than she'd thought, and it was so peaceful and quiet in the freezer. Bess and George were right. A few minutes of sleep would make them all feel better.

With a deep sigh, Nancy closed her eyes and rested her head on Bess's shoulder.

15

A Warm Reunion

The sound seemed to come from far away, as if someone was knocking on a door. Nancy nestled closer to Bess and tried to ignore it.

The sound was louder now, or maybe Nancy was more awake. *Bang! Bang! Bang!* With great difficulty, Nancy opened her eyes and tried to blink away the feeling that there was cotton stuffed in her head. Then she remembered where she was. The Frosty Freeze ice cream freezer.

Nancy's neck was stiff when she tried to turn her head to see Bess and George. The cousins were still huddled together, their eyes closed, their skin blue. It was hard to tell if they were even breathing. Fear started to pump adrenaline into Nancy's veins.

Bang! Bang! Bang! Finally Nancy was awake enough to realize what was going on. Someone was trying to save them. It must be the police, Nancy thought, a great sense of relief washing over her. They seemed to be knocking on all the doors in the building, waiting for an answer. What if they didn't realize the girls were in *this* freezer, since they'd gotten no response? Nancy had to get to the window in the door.

Her legs felt frozen solid. They wouldn't move. Nancy pounded on her thighs with her fists, trying to get some feeling into them. She barely felt her beating fists, but somehow she managed to rise to her feet.

The pounding had stopped. Was it too late?

"We're here!" Nancy cried as she shuffled toward the door. Behind her, Bess and George were motionless.

Nancy fell against the door and pressed her face to the glass. It was frosty, so she couldn't see out. She wiped the frost away, barely feeling the ice against her fingers.

There were several blue figures outside the door, talking to some people dressed in white. Nancy pounded against the glass, hoping they'd notice her.

Suddenly one of the blue figures looked up. It was Officer Brody. Nancy waved, hoping he could see her.

At first he didn't seem to react, so Nancy screamed and pounded as hard as she could on the window. Then Officer Brody gestured frantically to the others, who rushed over to the door. Nancy recognized Officers Rudinsky, Walker, and Daniel, as well as Chief McGinnis. There were also several people in white Frosty Freeze smocks.

"Stand back!" yelled Chief McGinnis, though his voice was muffled by the heavy door.

Nancy stepped backward toward Bess and George, who still hadn't moved. Was it too late for them? Nancy refused to believe it. Help had finally come. There had to be some way of reviving them.

"Wake up!" Nancy cried out, shaking her friends. "You have to get up!"

Bess mumbled something but didn't open her eyes. At least she was still alive. But what about George? Nancy placed a finger beneath George's nose to see if she was still breathing, but it was hard to tell.

Bang! Bang! Bang! Crash! The freezer door flew open, accompanied by the most welcome swoosh of warm air Nancy had ever felt. The police officers crowded in, already removing their jackets, which they threw over the shoulders of the three girls.

Looking back to see how her friends were doing, Nancy allowed herself to be led outside by Officer Walker. Officer Daniel had managed to get Bess to her feet, Nancy saw, but Officer Brody was having more difficulty with George.

"Wake up," he said, shaking her. "Come on!"

When she didn't respond, Brody gathered her up in his arms and raced her out to the hall.

"Gotta get some warm air into her lungs," he said, laying George on her back on the floor of the hallway. He pinched her nose with his fingers and leaned over her, breathing into her mouth. Then he sat up and pressed against her abdomen to make her exhale.

After he'd done this several times, George's eyelashes fluttered.

"She's alive!" Bess cried. With Officer Daniel's help, she knelt by her cousin. "George!" she cried. "Can you hear me?"

George's eyes opened at the sound of Bess's voice. Nancy breathed a deep sigh of relief.

"Good work," Chief McGinnis said to Officer Brody, who beamed with pride.

Nancy turned toward McGinnis, anxious to know how the police had found her and her friends. Her teeth were still chattering so hard she could barely get the words out.

Chief McGinnis understood. "Thompson made a big mistake," he told the girls. "He tried to drive the Frosty Freeze truck past security. When he didn't have proper identification, the guard tried to stop him, but he crashed through the gate. The guard immediately called the police. We already had four cars in the area, so we chased him and finally ran him off the road. He didn't want to tell us where you were, but we convinced him it was in his best interest to do so if he didn't want an even heavier sentence."

"Yeah," said Nancy. "I guess grand larceny, kidnapping, and attempted murder are enough to keep him in prison for a while."

"He's already warming a bench inside a cell at the station," McGinnis said. "Right next to Russell Brown." A look of concern came into the chief's eyes. "Speaking of warm, I think we should get you girls to the hospital right away to check you for frostbite. We found your friend George's car. If you give us the keys, we'll drive it over to the hospital so you can get home."

"Thanks," said Nancy gratefully. "I'll be okay, I think, but I'll feel better if a doctor takes a look at George."

"Oh, by the way," the police chief said, pulling a slim black pouch out of his jacket pocket. "Does this belong to one of you?"

"That's George's phone!" Nancy exclaimed. "She'll be so happy to get it back."

McGinnis handed the phone to Nancy. "You did a great job, as usual," he said. "What would we do without you?"

Nancy gave the chief a shaky smile. "Thank goodness you didn't have to find out."

Several hours later, Nancy, Bess, and George walked out of the hospital and into the warmth of the late afternoon sun.

"I can't believe how lucky we were," George said as they followed the walkway to her car. "A few more minutes in there, and we could have lost some fingers or toes."

"Or worse," Bess reminded her. Turning to Nancy, she said, "I guess I was wrong. Your luck hasn't run out yet. And I hope it never does!"

"I really thought it had this time," Nancy admitted, shaking her head. "And I was wrong, too. About

Lydia, I mean. She may not have been up front about her new business venture, but at least she's not a crook."

"Don't apologize," Bess said. "Even I was beginning to have my doubts about her."

"No one was above suspicion until the case was solved," George said. "Especially Kimberly Burton. I don't think she even realized she was a suspect, yet she seemed to be doing everything in her power to look suspicious. Makes you wonder about all the other crimes she was accused of, doesn't it?"

Nancy nodded. "That's what I was thinking," she agreed. "I wouldn't be surprised if she'd never committed a crime in her life. She probably just enjoys having a dangerous reputation."

"Maybe she's bored," Bess said. "I mean, living all alone inside that big house, with nothing to do all day but collect jewelry. No one would pay much attention to her if that was all she did. Being a suspected criminal must seem a lot more glamorous and exciting."

"I think you're right," Nancy said.

They reached the car, and George unlocked the door. "Maybe we should go lie in the sun for a while," she suggested as she got behind the wheel and reached over to unlock the passenger door.

"Okay," Bess said, climbing into the back seat. "But I think we should go out somewhere first. You know, to celebrate cracking the case."

"Hungry again, huh?" George asked her cousin.

"Always," said Bess, grinning.

"Sure, let's celebrate," Nancy agreed. "What do you feel like eating, Bess?"

"Ice cream!" said Bess without thinking.

For a moment, Nancy and George just stared at her. Then all three girls dissolved in laughter.

"That was just a reflex," Bess said. "Actually, it might take a while before I get my appetite back for Popsicles and Fudgsicles."

"I've got it!" Nancy exclaimed. "I know the perfect thing."

"What?" asked Bess and George together.

"Well, the temperature's eighty degrees," Nancy said, grinning impishly. "What do you say we all go out for some hot chocolate?"

NANCY DREW® MYSTERY STORIES By Carolyn Keene